BY *J. LYNN LOMBARD*

Copyright 2020

Cover Design Jay Aheer Simply Definedart.com

Edited by Sarah DeLong

Proofread by Katrina S.

This book is a work of fiction. References to real people, events, establishments, organizations, or locations are intended only to provide authenticity and are fictitious. All other characters and all incidents and dialogue are created in the author's imagination and are not real. Do not copy, reproduce or quote anything without the author's approval beforehand. The author reserves any and all rights to the book and the interaction between all characters involved.

WARNING,

This book contains mature content and is not suitable for everyone. If you enjoy reading about Alpha males along with action, adventure and drama, please continue. This book might give you triggers. If you can't handle death, torture or anything else along those lines, put the book down, back the fuck away and go play in the fields with your unicorns and rainbows. This book isn't intended for the weak of hearts.

If you're still here, Thank you for taking a chance on me and welcome to the Royal Bastards world....

ROYAL BASTARDS CODE

PROTECT: The club and your brothers come before anything else, and must be protected at all costs. **CLUB** is **FAMILY**.

RESPECT: Earn it & Give it. Respect club law. Respect the patch. Respect your brothers. Disrespect a member and there will be hell to pay.

HONOR: Being patched in is an honor, not a right. Your colors are sacred, not to be left alone, and **NEVER** let them touch the ground.

OL' LADIES: Never disrespect a member's or brother's Ol'Lady. **PERIOD.**

CHURCH is **MANDATORY.**

LOYALTY: Takes precedence over all, including well-being.

HONESTY: Never **LIE, CHEAT,** or **STEAL** from another member or the club.

TERRITORY: You are to respect your brother's property and follow their Chapter's club rules.

TRUST: Years to earn it...seconds to lose it.

NEVER RIDE OFF: Brothers do not abandon their family.

Prologue

Blayze

Sniveling and crying, snot and tears running down his face, this low-ranking member of Los Demons is about to take his last breath. He was caught snooping around the Royal Bastards Clubhouse earlier today. Torch, our Enforcer, has been having too much fun with him for the past six hours. Between begging for his life and cursing us all to hell, he hasn't told us jack shit on why he was there. Now, we're out on an abandoned dead-end road and he's on his knees in the dirt. The headlights of everyone's bikes make a circle around the sorry piece of shit.

"I'm gonna ask you one more time, Punta. Why are you here?" Capone, the President of Royal Bastards MC, Los Angeles Chapter and my best friend asks him. His real name is Derek but because of his badass looks and his jet-black hair, the old Prez, Chains, called him Capone when he was little and the nickname stuck ever since.

"No entiendo." *No understand.* Los Demons sobs through his tears and snot.

"Oh, you understand all right," Capone taunts, leaning right into his face. "Because when I end your life, I'm going to fuck your sister." The man growls low and tries to head-butt Capone, but he steps back laughing. "Told you he understood English."

Capone cracks his neck from side to side. His deadly black eyes glare at our captive. His leather cut with our club logo, creaks under the move. "Pendejo, I'm going to ask you one more time. Why are the Los Demons snooping around my club?"

"Vete a la Merida," *Fuck you.* He growls.

Capone smirks and nods his head to Torch, "Have fun. I've got better things to do." Capone turns on his heels and steps away. I immediately follow him into the pitch-black night. Screams pierce the air and a shiver races down my spine. The Los Demon breathed his last breath.

Once we're away from the area and near where the two of us parked our bikes, Capone lights up a smoke and slows down. "Blayze, I'll need you and Bear to keep watch over the next few days. Something tells me we haven't seen the last of Los Demons."

"You got it, Prez," I respond, lighting up my cigarette. I inhale the nicotine deep into my lungs. "What are your thoughts?"

Capone stares out into the deserted valley sitting high in the mountains on the outskirts of Los Angeles. The property our Chapter of the Royal Bastards MC owns is perfect for what we do. We're the elite one-percenters, riding the line of legal and illegal. We run everything from guns, to drugs, to money laundering. Some of our legal businesses such as the sanctioned fighting ring, bars and porn business keeps us off the cop's radar. But with Los Demons sniffing around today, something big is going down. Something we're not seeing.

"I'm thinking, Los Demons want to take over our territory. We'll send them a message with that piece of shit." Capone grins. A look passes through his eyes. He enjoys this shit. Which I don't blame him. There's something that embeds deep into your soul when you become the judge, jury and executioner rolled into one.

One final scream pierces the air, causing the birds roosting in the trees to take flight. Capone stomps his cigarette out under his boot and mounts his bike. I do the same and the two of us ride back to the clubhouse. My thoughts are on what our next move will be if Los Demons show up again. We can keep torturing and tormenting them, or we can go on the offense and go after them. Make them stop now before one of our own gets caught in the crosshairs. And by one of our own, I'm thinking about a sexy as hell porn queen, Monica. Capone's sister. From her long lean legs which wrap perfectly around my waist, to her shoulder length dark hair I can grab, Monica consumes my every thought. I won't make a move on her because she's Capone's little sister, but I sure as hell will fantasize about the things I can do to her.

Chapter 1

Blayze

The rumble of my Harley Davidson Deluxe Review-First Ride pierces the quiet night. Capone and I follow the road that leads to a long driveway and ride up to a chain-link fence surrounding a huge cement building that used to be a warehouse at one time but now belongs to the Royal Bastards MC. There's a guard shack to the left in front of the fence unmanned. The only way in or out of this place is through the rolling gates. Unless you want to be a fucking idiot like the now dead guy for Los Demons and climb the fence. We set security cameras up in every corner of the building and the blind spot along the fence moving with us on motion sensors. Capone and I stand idle until the gates to our clubhouse roll open. Once Tiny sees us from his spot at the over watch, he hits a button and the gate buzzes and creaks, allowing us inside. Capone and I ride to the left of the gates, past the full parking lot and roll up to the white garage doors. He hits a button on his bike and the door rolls up. We pull inside and park our bikes side by side, while the garage door closes behind us. The fluorescent lights turn on the motion sensors detecting our movements.

I remove my helmet, hanging it on the handlebars and light up a smoke. The nicotine burns my lungs and relaxes me. Capone climbs off his bike, removes his helmet and places it on the backseat. "I need you to find Monica and keep a close eye on her."

Capone might not admit to caring about his sister, but we all know he does. Sometimes he cares too much and Monica being on the receiving end gets pissed. She's an independent woman determined to make it in our world without relying on her brother. All he wants to do is protect her. In his mind, he failed her when he sent her to Detroit and Steam, the President of Savage Saints, MC Detroit caught up with her. We didn't know Chains, our old President, knew Steam. We were in the middle of a turf war where tides were turning, and Monica was trapped in the crosshairs. Capone thought it was safer for her to be there, but it wasn't. Steam figured out who she was and tried to kill her. He caught her, but Monica's stubborn ass refused to succumb to him. She still carries the emotional and physicals scars.

"Aye, Prez. Consider it done. I won't let her out of my sight." I reply, stomping my smoke out.

I climb off my bike and together we walk down the long corridor leading deep into the clubhouse. We enter the common room together. To the left are the pool tables and dartboards. Some brothers who didn't make the run with us tonight are there, hitting on the club bunnies and they're soaking up the attention. To the right are a few couches and chairs set up in front of a seventy-inch-widescreen TV. The noise from the Xbox drowns out talking as people are gathering around it and taking bets as a prospect and Trigger, our Treasurer, battle it out in a boxing match.

To the back of the common room is another prospect tending the bar. He's slinging drinks as fast as he can with a white towel thrown over his shoulder. Behind the bar is our club logo etched in mirrored glass. Twenty-six Chapters range from the east coast starting in Boston,

MA; NYC; Baltimore, MD, all the way south to Miami, FL then across the US through Georgia, Mississippi, Louisiana, Tennessee, Kentucky, Missouri, West Virginia, Michigan, Colorado, Nebraska, Texas, to the west coast in Arizona, California, Nevada and Alaska. Twenty-six Chapters all over the US. If any one of them needs anything, we drop what we're doing and go in a heartbeat. Loyalty to the Club goes before everything else. It doesn't matter if you're balls deep in your Ol' Lady on your honeymoon in Cavo. If a Chapter needs help, you are there with no hesitation.

A pair of long, sun-kissed slender legs sitting at the bar catches my attention. My eyes trail up the pair of legs to an ass perfect for squeezing, following a slender back, slightly arched, and curly dark hair with blonde highlights. She tilts her head to the side and Monica pins me with a cool gaze in her honey brown eyes. She lifts the beer bottle to her plump, red lips and takes a long pull. Watching her lick her lips, everyone's voices fade to the background. It's just the two of us around as I watch her seductively shift on the bar stool. She turns her body, so her back is to the bar and I get a full view of her luscious rack in a red, tight-fitting dress. Monica crosses one leg over the other and pops her chest out a little. My jeans tighten. This woman will be the death of me if I can't get her to see how good we fit together. As long as her brother doesn't kill me first.

I take one step in front of the other, my eyes set on my prey. Monica's smoky eyes are hooded with desire, the closer I get. I adjust the raging hard-on and she smirks. She knows what she does to me and loves to be a tease. One day, very soon, she'll be begging me to take her over the edge.

A warm hand wraps around my bicep, bursting the seductive bubble Monica and I are in and she stiffens on her seat, swinging back around to face the bar. I look down and see Samantha's purple nails digging into my skin. Her lavender scent surrounding me, making me stifle a gag.

"Can we talk?" Sam bats her green eyes at me. She is the club bitch. Always wanting her way and throws a fit when she doesn't get it. She can make your life a living hell if you don't oblige.

"What do you want, Sam?" I growl low in my throat. The raging hard-on I had disappears from her voice alone.

"I just want to talk to you." Sam whines. She pushes her blonde hair with purple streaks back, tucking it behind her ears. Some guys might enjoy her company, but I don't. I can't stand the bitch and she knows this.

"I'm busy." I try to pull her claws from my arm, but she won't let go. If anything, she digs deeper into my skin. I'm surprised I don't see blood blooming from under her nails. "Club business, Sam. Move along to another brother who I'm sure will give you the attention you're seeking. That isn't me. Never has been. Never will be." I finally get her claws off my bicep and turn back to the bar.

Monica is gone. Nowhere in sight. I search with my eyes, all over the common room and she's not in here. Sam is still standing next to me batting her eyes and licking her lips. The look is disgusting.

"Looks like your *business* disappeared on you." Samantha runs her fingers up my cut. "I can be the business you need to attend to. Not some stuck-up little bitch who thinks she's better than the rest of us."

Rage simmers below my skin. I grab her hand on my cut and put just enough pressure to make Samantha squeal. I rarely put my hands on a woman, but she's pushed my last nerve. I pull her in close and she struggles before relaxing against my brutal grip. She's one of the women who like it rough. A smile graces her lips and Sam purrs with delight. She thinks I will fuck her now, and I use that to my advantage.

I lean in real close, pressing my nose against the shell of her ear. "If you ever touch me again, I will fucking kill you. I never and won't ever want you. Get that through your thick skull. There will never be a thing between us." I release her hand and she stumbles a little in her six inch stilettos. "Now get the fuck away from me before you regret getting on my bad side." Samantha scrambles away fast, looking for refuge in another's arms. Thank fuck she finally gets the hint.

I search each room in the back of the common room. These rooms are for the club brothers and their families when we are on lockdown. Each room is set up for a family ranging from two to four people, in case we needed a comfortable place for them to stay in. Coming up empty, I continue my search. Monica has to be around here somewhere. Why does she make my job harder than it has to be?

I head out the back door and cross the parking lot in the back of the clubhouse. It's secluded and dark back here. The flood lights set up around the perimeter give off just enough light to see the path toward the gym. The warm summer night wraps around me. Grunting noises catch my attention toward the gym. I close the distance with quick steps. I push open the metal door and search the dark room not seeing Monica. I spot a faint light coming from the back of the gym. I quietly make my way toward the light and hear more grunting, followed by sobs that break my heart into a million pieces. I know that sob from anywhere. I've heard it and soothed it for months after Monica's attack in Detroit. She's spiraling and I need to be here to help build her back up. It's not a job for me, but something I want to do. I want to be here when she needs me.

I lean against the doorway leading into the boxing room and let her get it all out. Sometimes I can't interfere. If I do, it makes her breakdown even worse. She'll lash out at me instead of battling the demons in her mind. I watch as she hits a big bag with everything she has. In her skin-tight red dress and no heels, it's sexy as fuck. Her bare feet are in the fighter stance I taught her years ago. Sweat beads on her brow and her curly hair is plastered to her tear-stained face.

Monica stops swinging at the bag and collapses onto the mats, sobbing. I hurry over to her and wrap her body into my arms. At first, she fights my embrace, then her body relaxes against mine.

"I'm sorry, Bug. So sorry this happened to you." I smooth her hair out of her face and Monica looks up at me with tears in her eyes.

"It's not your fault, Xander." Monica is the only one who can get away with calling me by my real name and not my road name, Blayze.

I wipe the tears from her cheeks and press my lips against her forehead. "What set you off?"

"Honestly? I have no idea. I was doing fine until that skank," She's referring to Sam. "Had her hands all over you."

"You know there's nothing going on right?"

"Yeah, I know. But then I think about what she can give you that I can't and I spiral."

"The only thing she can give me that you can't is an STD. That woman is nasty." I shiver at the thought. Monica laughs a little, showing me we're on the right path, fighting from the darkness consuming her.

"What if one day, we take this," She points between us, "Whatever we have further and you want kids? I can't give you that. That choice was taken away from me."

"Bug, I know that. And it doesn't matter. Whatever is between us," I point between the two of us, mimicking her. "Is between us. If we take this further and someday want kids, we can adopt. There are plenty of things we can do. But let's not worry about that right now. Right now, I need to keep you safe. You're not to leave my sight until further notice and I don't want it any other way."

Monica releases a deep sigh and snuggles into my arms. Her small frame fits perfectly against my large one. The scent of jasmine and vanilla, everything that makes Monica, fills my nose and I savor it. She runs a finger along the tattoos on my arm marking my skin.

"What are we doing, Xander? Why are you here?" Monica's voice is quiet in the large room.

"I'm here because I want to be. Your brother wants full protection on you after some shit we found out earlier, but that doesn't matter because I'm wherever you are. Always have been, Bug." I want to kiss her. I want to close the distance between us and ravish her lips with my own. Then I want to command her body with mine. But it's not the right time. Not after an episode. "C'mon, Bug. You're staying with me tonight."

I stand up and help Monica to her feet. She pushes her body against mine and wraps her arms around my waist, resting her head against my chest. "Thank you, Xander."

An unspoken moment passes between us and I latch onto it with both hands. I return her embrace, loving the way she fits perfectly against me. Monica and I have known each other since we were teenagers. Her brother Capone and I have been inseparable since I came into the Royal Bastards at fifteen. She was the one I always wanted but never pursued. She was always out of my league; good grades in high school, popular, captain of the cheer squad. And I was one of the troublemakers. Always fighting, being suspended and finally they kicked me out for good my senior year. Most of the trouble I was in, was because of this woman in my arms. I've always protected her and always will.

I cup the sides of her face with my large hands and lean close so our lips are inches apart. "I will always protect you and keep you safe." Monica's breath picks up and she darts her tongue out to lick her lips. My jeans tighten. "I might have failed once before, but I won't fail you again."

"Kiss me, Xander. Make me forget and give me what you can." Monica whispers against my lips.

That's all the permission I need. My mouth crashes down onto hers and she opens her lips, giving me access. I plunge my tongue into her mouth and savor Monica's flavor on my lips. She battles mine, back and forth. It's wet, it's raw, it's real. It's who we are. I break the kiss and rest my forehead against hers, breathing hard. Monica grips my cut in her small hands trying to get her bearing back.

A loud crack echoes through the gym and we jump apart. I pull my gun out from my cut and tuck Monica behind me, protecting her. Together, we walk quietly toward the noise. Once we leave the boxing area, it's dark. I didn't flip any lights on when I was trying to find her. Now, I wish I did. The crack echoes again the closer we get to the entrance.

The front door swings open and closed with the wind. Someone was in here watching us. I'll guaran-fucking-tee it. I know I closed that door when I came in here. With my heart pounding against my chest and Monica's fingers clutching my back pocket, I open the door and look around. There's no one out here anymore. Whoever it was is long gone. We cross the parking lot in hurried steps and enter the back door.

I turn to Monica, "Get to my room and lock the door. Do not open it for anyone."

"Where are you going?" Her voice trembles with fear.

"I need to see Capone. Then I'll be right behind you."

She hurries off toward my room and when she's out of sight, I make my way to Capone's office. I knock on the oak door and wait for him to answer. Capone yanks open the door, tucking his white t-shirt in his jeans and motions for me to enter. A club bunny scurries out of his office, covering her chest with her shirt. Capone buckles his belt and takes a seat in the leather chair behind his desk. Sweat and sex linger in the room and I raise an eyebrow. He shrugs and leans back in the chair, resting his hands behind his head.

"What's up, Blayze."

"Someone was in the gym with Monica and me. They took off before I could see who it was." I respond taking a seat in front of his desk. It's probably the most sanitized seat in the room. I'd hate to shine a black light on the leather sofa, his desk or chair. I don't tell him about the kiss that distracted me from knowing who was around.

Capone leans forward in his chair and steeples his hands on his desk. The satisfied look he had on his face when I came in here is long gone. "Who do you think it was?"

"I don't know. It couldn't have been the ass fucker John. He hasn't been here since Savage Saints came into town and I made Monica go with me."

"Do you think whoever it was is out to hurt her or scare the fuck out of her?"

"I'm thinking they want to scare her."

"But why? What has she done?" Capone's brow scrunches in confusion. Our suspects are limited to our brothers and the club bunnies. Those are the only ones allowed in our clubhouse.

"Monica hasn't done a fucking thing to anyone," I snarl. "Fuck me. I have an idea who it could be." All the color drains from my face and my body is vibrating with rage.

"Who? I'll punish them for scaring my sister." Capone's jaw ticks with fury.

"Samantha. She came on to me tonight and was pissed I didn't take her up on her advances."

"I'll send Bear to find the bitch. If it was her, she won't like fucking with my sister." Capone slams his fist on his desk causing the things on it to rattle and stands up. He motions with his head for me to leave.

Bear is the Royal Bastards Sargent at Arms. He's a big burly man with tree branches for limbs and his neck is as big as my thigh. His real name is Mark Jacobs. He got the nickname Bear because even with his tough exterior, he's a teddy bear with the women in the club. He's one of the most respectful men around. He loves the attention the women give him and is a gentle giant thanks to his mama, a well-known stripper, who taught her boy at a young age how to treat a lady. Something happened to her when he was little and no one besides Capone knows what it is. When he is ready to share, he will.

I stand up quickly from my seat and walk toward the door. Capone rests his hand on my shoulder, "Stay with Monica at all times. I'll search around and see what I can figure out. Don't let her out of your sight."

"I won't, Prez. Thanks."

"Blayze," Capone calls my name when I walk out the door. I turn in his direction. "You're the only one I trust to keep my sister safe. Don't let me down."

"I won't. I promise on my patch, Monica will have my full attention." In more ways than what Capone wants or thinks. She's always had my protection and always will. He'd maim my balls if he knew what kind of protection I wanted to give his sister.

"Good. I'll see you in the morning." Capone walks away, into the rowdy crowd in the common room before I can answer.

Turning, I make my way down the dark corridor toward my bedroom. I will find out what in the hell is going on one way or another. I will discover who's after Monica and why. I will find out who's trying to bring my club down. I will not stop until I have the answers I need.

Chapter 2

Monica

I unlock Xander's door with the key he gave me months ago when I came back from Detroit and slip inside. Glancing around his room, I'm floored with memories of what's happened to me over the past few years. I've spent months recovering from what Steam and Chains did to me and Xander's room was the only safety I could find.

Nightmares of that awful night plague my sleep. Every time I close my eyes, if I'm not with Xander, I can still feel the blade of Chains' knife rip into my stomach. I can still feel the sweat dripping from their bodies as they beat me to within inches of my life. I can still smell the blood spilling from my body as I fight with everything I have. Capone, my brother, and the rest of the Royal Bastards MC took care of Chains when they found me recovering in another tenant's apartment. I didn't ask how or where. It's not my place. They couldn't touch Steam unless they had permission so that asshole is still out there wreaking havoc on the other Savage Saints members and they don't even know about it. When I'm in this room and with Xander, the nightmares stay away. I can't do this without him. I can't get past it all without him by my side. Xander knows everything I've been through, everything I've lost and he still looks at me with lust in his deep green eyes, taking my breath away.

We've been playing the dangerous game of cat-and-mouse for years. I'm always the mouse, scurrying away from the big bad cat. I'm tired of hiding. I want him like I've never wanted a man before. He'd captured my heart the moment his boots hit the halls of our high school. With his leather jacket and bad boy attitude, I was a goner. Xander's been best friends with my brother Derek, or what the club calls him, Capone, and won't take our relationship further because of him. He doesn't want to disappoint Capone by hurting me. But he doesn't realize, he is hurting me by not doing anything. So, instead of wallowing in self-pity, I'm ready to take what I want. I'm ready to bare my soul, scars and all to get the man I've always wanted.

I shimmy out of the tight dress I wore and leave it on the floor along with my high heels. I make my way to the bathroom in just my bra and panties. Flipping on the light, I take a long look at myself in the mirror above the sink. I take the time to fix my hair and apply makeup to cover the dark bags under my eyes just to catch Xander's attention. This isn't who I am, so why am I trying to hide my true self with this shit? I turn on the hot water and scrub my face clean. I pop my contacts out and put on my black framed glasses resting on Xander's countertop. I run the brush through my hair and pull it up in a ponytail.

Feeling more like myself, I take another glance in the mirror. The woman staring back at me doesn't hide from her scars. I don't even flinch anymore when I see the damage done to my body. The crisscross scars lining my abdomen don't make me weep anymore. If anything, they strengthen me. Stronger to fight for what I want. Stronger to prove that I can still live my life even if the one thing I wanted more than anything was taken away from me. Now, I need to take that strength and pour it into getting the man I want. The man who creates a need between my legs. The man who makes my desire burn.

The doorknob jiggles, pulling me out of my head. I quickly slip on Xander's black Royal Bastards t-shirt sitting on the counter and lean against the door frame separating the bathroom from the bedroom. Adjusting the glasses perched on my nose, I cross my arms over my chest and wait. The bedroom door opens and Xander walks inside, closing it quietly behind him. His head is down so he doesn't notice me standing here right away. The air escapes my lungs as I stare at his muscular frame. His inked arm muscles bulge with strength as he sets his gun, wallet and chain attached to his belt on the dresser. His ass is perfect for squeezing while he drives hard into me. Damn, I'm all hot and bothered and all he did was walk into the room.

Xander turns around and spots me. A smile graces his full lips I want to kiss so badly again, I can taste his mouthwatering flavor. His blonde hair is shaggy and brushing against his shoulders and his light goatee is making me squirm when I think about what it can do between my legs.

"Everything OK with Capone?" I ask, my voice is husky with a need and want I haven't had in a long time. Not since the attack.

"Yeah, Bug. Everything will be fine." Xander is hiding something. I can see it in his eyes.

"What aren't you telling me? Come on Xander, after everything I've been through, I have a right to know." I push off the door frame and sit in the middle of the bed, crossing my legs.

Xander watches me and licks his lips as his eyes trail up my bare legs to my full breasts, ready for attention. "Nothing, Bug." He replies finally meeting my eyes. "We'll have a visitor tomorrow at the studio."

"Who?" I ask raising an eyebrow. Since returning from Detroit, I'm the porn queen. I direct porn for the club and I'm great at my job. I don't fuck the actors or actresses. I go to the studio, do the job and go home. Lately, it's been grating on my nerves because my ex, John James, demands to be there, hoping I'll give him another chance. Since he's shown his true colors when the Savage Saints came looking for me, I'll never give him the time of day nor will I let him back into my life. He's a weasel dick asshole looking to get into my panties. These panties only come off for one man. I've never let J.J. in and never will.

"F.O.C.U.S., from our NYC Chapter. He's stopping in really quick to talk to me about some club business." Xander shrugs off his Royal Bastards cut and carefully drapes it over the chair in the corner. He pulls his white Royal Bastards t-shirt over his head and drops it on the floor. My mouth waters from the move. Xander is standing in front of me in nothing but his low hanging jeans, showing his washboard abs that I'm itching to run my fingers over and lick every curve and crevice, the sexy V leading to a place I want more than anything right now.

I uncross my legs, keeping eye contact with him and strut my way over to where he's standing. Placing my hands on his stomach, his body shivers from my touch. I trail my nails up his abs over his shoulders and wrap my arms around Xander's neck. He places his big hands around my waist, pulling me close. His nose trails up my neck followed by his tongue. Xander's palms squeeze my ass, pulling me closer to him. We're now chest to chest.

"What are we doing, Bug?" He breathes into my hair.

"Taking what we both want, Blayze." I pant. His hardness presses into my stomach making my panties wet with desire. "Do you want me?"

"More than I should." Xander's lips crash down onto mine taking my breath away. He runs his tongue along the seam of my lips and I open them allowing him entrance. A moan vibrates from the back of my throat. He squeezes my ass as my nails dig into his hair. Want, lust and need are heavy in the air. I want him. I crave all of him. I need him to quench this lust burning through my body.

"Are you wet for me, Bug?" Xander pants against my lips.

"Only for you," I answer honestly. I cup his length through his jeans and press against it with the palm of my hand.

Xander holds onto my shoulders and looks me directly in the eyes. "We need to make sure this is what we both want. If we take this step and you're not ready, Capone will cut off my dick and shove it down my throat. I'm kind of attached to it."

I pull my hand away and move to the middle of the bed. I take a deep breath before yanking his t-shirt over my head, exposing my scars. "If my trust in showing you these doesn't tell you I'm ready, then you aren't ready. No one has seen these and how disfigured it's made me. No one knows how deep these scars really run." I turn to face Xander. His eyes are trailing up and down my body, hooded with desire. "If I didn't want this next step with you, I wouldn't be here."

Xander kicks off his boots, quickly unbuckles his jeans and drops them to the floor. He crawls his way over to me in the middle of the bed and cups my cheeks. His mouth captures mine in a ravishing kiss that takes my breath away. He scoops me up so my legs are straddling his waist and gently lays me down. He trails his tongue down the column of my neck and lavishes one aching breast while his fingers pinch and squeeze my other one. My hips buck up into him wanting more.

"Please, Xander." I pant into the room. He goes further down my body and gently kisses each scar marring my body.

"So, beautiful," Xander rumbles against my skin. He moves further down and yanks my black panties off in one move, exposing me fully to him. He sits back on his heels, looking at me. His green eyes are hooded with desire. He pulls off his boxers, exposing himself to me and my mouth waters at the sigh. I want to run my tongue over his flesh and take him deep into my mouth. I lick my lips and a smirk appears on Xander's face.

"Like what you see, Bug?" I nod my head. No words will form in my head. He strokes himself a few times and turns his attention to my body. He leans forward and kisses his way up my right leg before stopping. Xander darts his tongue out, making me moan. "That's it, Monica, let go. I'll catch you." I yank on his hair, pulling his body up mine.

"Give it to me, Blayze." I moan. Irritation flashes in Xander's eyes and I release a sexy laugh. I only call him Blayze when I want to get his fire burning. He'd rather me call him by his God given name, not his road name unless we're around the rest of his brothers, then it's rude not to call him by his road name. He's finally picking up on what I'm doing and smirks. "I need you inside of me."

I hook my legs around his waist and push his body close to mine. "Are you sure, Monica?"

"I'm positive, Xander. Make me yours." I've never meant the words more than I do at this moment. I want to be his Ol' Lady. I want everything about him. The darkness he lives in, the secrets he carries. I want it all.

I'm ready for him to break through the barriers I've raised and crash down my walls. I'm ready to feel our connection on a deeper level. Relief floods through my body as he tears down the walls I've surrounded myself with. Once Xander's fully inside, he covers me with his body and moves his hips, I lose my mind, clawing at his back, pulling him closer. His mouth captures mine and his tongue plunges inside. I moan into his mouth and his hips buck faster, driving into me. My body responds to his, sending me higher and higher into the atmosphere. My orgasm is within reach when Xander breaks our soul-stealing kiss.

"Give me all of you, Monica." He demands and I respond, flying high.

"Fuck, Xander, I'm coming." I pant. We're a mess of sweat, tongues and lips and I'm loving our beautiful mess. Xander grunts and my name falls from his lips as he finds his release.

"Holy, fuck." Falls from Xander's lips. He's still above me, holding himself up on his elbows. He gently kisses me and I breathe him in.

"Hmmm…" That's all I can get out. My mind is still mush and my body is relaxed. Xander rolls off, pulling me with him. His strong arm wraps around my shoulders and I rest my head on his chest. His heart is beating hard against my ear, lulling me to sleep. For once in my life, I don't think about tomorrow or the future. I think about this moment right here, right now.

"Thank you, Xander. For giving me what I needed." I drift off into a deep sleep, free from the nightmares plaguing my mind.

Chapter 3

Blayze

The sun streams through the curtains of my bedroom window, waking me from a deep slumber. Capone and I are the only ones with rooms on the outer edge of the clubhouse. The rest of the rooms are deep inside, safe from anyone breaking in. We prefer it this way to keep our members and their families protected.

Monica is still sleeping on my chest. Her breathing is deep and even. Memories from last night come back to me in my groggy state and a smile graces my lips. We finally went past the barriers we built around ourselves and gave each other something we both needed and craved. Love. I love this woman with everything I have and will let no one harm her again.

A loud thump outside my bedroom door clears the fogginess of sleep from my brain. We're still on alert and I let my guard down last night. When I'm with Monica, everything else takes a back burner, and I can't be doing that. In order to keep her safe, I need to be aware of everything and everyone around me.

"Monica," I whisper. She moves and rubs her leg against my growing erection. "Don't make a sound. I'll be right back." I lightly kiss the side of her head and climb out of bed. I find my boxers on the floor and slip them on quietly. Another thump followed by a loud crack sounds again right outside my bedroom door. I hurry to my dresser and grab my gun. With my finger on the trigger and my other hand on the doorknob, I unlock it and twist. Yanking the door open fast I aim the barrel of my .45 caliber Smith & Wesson at the temple of whoever's making that noise right outside my door.

"Don't move, motherfucker or I'll blow your brains out." The guy on the other side of my door raises his arms and drops the baseball bat in his hands. "What the fuck do you think you're doing?"

"I'm trying to get the rat," his voice trembles.

"There are no fucking rats in here. I think you're trying to scare my girl." I click the safety off my gun. "Who the fuck are you and tell me why I shouldn't kill you right here."

Stomping boots down the hallway draws my attention away from the trembling guy and Capone comes flying down the hallway. "Blayze, don't," Capone commands. "That's Jezebelle's kid. Apparently, the other boys dared him to chase a non-existent rat down this hallway to get him into trouble."

I lower my gun and glare at the kid. "This true?"

The boy turns around with tears in his eyes, nodding his head. Now that I really look at him, he's just a teenager. Tall and skinny with acne all teenagers get. "Yes. They made me do it. Told me if I didn't, they would beat me up." Jezebelle is one of the porn stars for Royal Bastards. Her and Derange, the Club's Tail Runner, have had an on and off thing for the past few years. She won't tell us who her kids' dad is and we don't ask.

Staring into his brown eyes, I talk to him man to man. "Next time those boys want you to do something, remember this day. You're lucky I didn't shoot your ass then ask questions." I put my gun on my dresser and check on Monica. She isn't in bed anymore, but the bathroom door is closed. "Get out of here little dude."

"Yes, Blayze." The hopeful look in his chocolate eyes pierces into my soul.

"Stand the fuck up for yourself. If you know it's wrong, don't fucking do it. Don't let those little assholes force you into doing something that could get you killed."

"Yes, Sir. Thank you, Sir." He scurries off in the direction that Capone came from. Once he's out of sight I relax and open my door for Capone to come inside.

He strolls in and sits in the chair in the corner of my room. His eyebrows raise at the messy bed and I internally groan. Fuck me.

"Where's my sister?"

"In the bathroom," I answer, sitting on the edge of the bed and slide my jeans on.

"Didn't I tell you to protect her at all costs, not fuck her?" Capone is pissed. The tick of his jaw is the only sign he's showing, but I can see it in his dark eyes.

I shrug. I'm caught and no point in denying it. "Can't help who you fall for, Prez. We've been skirting around the attraction for years. And I wouldn't change last night for anything."

"That's the first time the two of you have been together?" Capone asks, baffled.

"Yup," I answer popping the P. I'm really uncomfortable talking to him about my sex life, but Capone is the type that doesn't give a shit how uncomfortable you are. If he has questions, he will ask.

"So, you two are a thing now? Do I need to remind you what she's been through?" Capone leans forward and rests his elbows on his knees.

Monica comes out of the bathroom and sits next to me on the bed. I drape an arm around her shoulders. She answers him before I can. "Yes. We're a thing now. Both of us have been wanting it for a while but your overbearing big brother asshole ways have stopped me from taking what I want."

"Well, I'll leave you two alone. Remember about the meeting this morning, Blayze. Don't be late. F.O.C.U.S. and some of the NYC members only have a few minutes." Capone rises from the chair, crosses the room in a few quick strides and pauses at the door. "Blayze, I'm actually happy Monica chose you. Now, I don't have to beat the shit out of her next boyfriend, since I've done that once before." We chuckle remembering the night we got into a scuffle. Monica's head ping pongs between the two of us and shakes it. We were both teenagers, drunk and had it out over her once before. He didn't beat me up, but I let him think he did. Capone turns around and pins me with a glare in his black eyes. "Don't hurt her."

"I swear, I'm not planning on it. She's all I need." I keep his gaze until he turns around and walks out the door, closing it behind him.

"Did you really mean all of that?" Monica asks, staring at me. A genuine smile graces her full lips.

"Every word, Bug. You're all I've wanted and all I'll ever need." I kiss the top of her forehead and she stands up. "Now, we need to get to the studio before we're late." I swat her ass and she yelps. I rise from the bed and stalk over to her. The top of her curly dark hair comes to my chin. I pull Monica into my arms and she comes willingly.

"Thought we had to leave?" Monica asks, wrapping her arms around my waist.

"In a minute," I answer, holding her close. She peers up at me through her long lashes. We stand in the middle of my bedroom, just watching each other. Something's shifting between us and I'm powerless to stop it.

"Let's go. You know how those porn stars are when their producer is late." Monica gives me a sassy smile that lights up her brown eyes.

I kiss her gently on the lips, then release her to finish getting dressed. I slide on a clean, black Royal Bastards MC t-shirt and slip on my cut. Holstering my .45 caliber and putting my wallet in my back pocket, I turn. "Ready?"

"Yeah, let's make some porn." There's something off with Monica. I can tell the way her eyes aren't lighting up with excitement.

"Hey, what's wrong?"

"Nothing." Monica casts her eyes down to the carpet and fidgets with her Royal Bastards tank top. I know she's lying. She only fidgets when she's lying or nervous.

"Bug, look at me," I command. She sighs and lifts her eyes to meet mine. "What's going on?"

"I'm just worried," Monica confesses.

"Worried about what? Come on. It's me and you now. Stop bottling up your feelings and tell me so I can fix it." I reach her in two quick strides.

"John. I'm worried how he's going to react when he realizes we're together." The worry in her voice is clear. Monica doesn't enjoy pissing people off or thinking anyone hates her. She's suffered so much hate from Chains. Capone and I did what we could to shield her from his wrath. Now that he's gone, our lives are easier but she's right.

"Don't worry about that pencil dick motherfucker. He gives you any trouble, you kick his weasel dick ass." I brush Monica's hair from her face. "What did you see in him anyway?" I genuinely want to know. I could never figure out what she saw in him. With his brown hair slicked back, always wearing white wife beater tank tops, a pair of stone-washed jeans and several gold chains around his neck, he's a wanna-be thug trying to be king shit in Venice Beach.

"Honestly? He was the total opposite from you. He filled the void of not having you with me. Trust me, I never let him touch me, but made him want me. I feel horrible for leading him on these past few months and his obsession is borderline creepy." A smile forms on my lips. "What the hell are you smiling for, Blayze?"

"He is totally opposite from me. I can't help it. I'm the king shit who has the girl." Pride fills my voice. I lean down so our lips are a hair's breadth away. "Now, let's show him who you belong to." My mouth crashes down onto Monica's with an unforgiving force. She moans and opens her lips. I slip my tongue inside and devour every inch of her hot, wet mouth. Monica breaks the kiss, breathing heavily. Her full breasts rise and fall with every inhale and exhale. I can't help but look down between the valley of her breasts. My mouth waters, craving to suck, lick and nibble on each one until she's compliant from my touch.

"We need to go." Monica's voice is husky with want and need.

I grab Monica's hand, adjust my aching dick with the other and together we leave the sanctuary of my bedroom. I lock the door behind us and settle my arm over her shoulders, pulling her next to me, showing the club she's mine. They already knew, but now it's official. Monica is mine.

Chapter 4

Monica

The ride on Blayze's bike over to my studio in Venice Beach was cathartic. With my body wrapped around his, we fell into a groove. A quiet understanding that this is where I'm meant to be. I'm supposed to be on the back of his Harley. I'm meant to be by his side. No matter what. And to me, that means so much.

Blayze pulls into the parking spot in front of the non-descript white-washed building, puts his kickstand down and turns off his bike. We sit in silence for a few moments. My arms wrapped around his waist, my head resting on his cut. I hate wearing a helmet, even if it's a half-helmet but the California laws tell me I need to. And if I got onto any bike without one, Blayze would have a fit. I've tried it before when I used to ride.

When we were teenagers, Derek taught me how to ride without Chains knowing so I could escape the hell I was in. Chains was an old school President who thought a woman in an MC meant she spread her legs when a brother wanted and to fix them food when they demanded. It was hell living there, but I had no choice. Mine and Capone's mother was in too deep with Chains, she couldn't leave. She did a lot of shady shit in the MC and even made Chains think Capone was his. When the truth came out that Capone wasn't Chains' son, it was too late. Everyone respected him and followed his words. When war broke out inside the club, only a few sided with Chains and the rest went with Capone. He sent me away to stay in Detroit to keep me out of harm's way, but Chains found me through Steam, the Savage Saints MC, Detroit Chapter's President. Bits and pieces of that night are still missing from my memory. The only thing I remember is the slice of their blade on my skin and the pain from their fists raining down blows on my face and body.

I haven't been the same after that dreadful night. I was seeing a man named Blayde. He was a newly patched in member of Savage Saints, Detroit. We had a big fight after some guy made a pass at me. I didn't want violence and Blayde scared the little shit so bad, I think he pissed himself. We went back to my apartment, fucked and then had a huge fight. I was projecting my feelings for Blayze to Blayde. I missed him terribly the year I was in hiding. Blayde fit the bill for a badass biker to fill the void of not having Blayze. Little did anyone know, while I was in hiding, I was getting information for Capone to use against Chains. He set me up as a stripper for Deadly Sins Club and found out Steam, the President of Savage Saints, Detroit had the mayor in his back pocket. I kept that secret for a long time. It ate away at who I was. The secret about Blayde's best friend, Kayne's father's death, tortured my heart and soul.

Blayze taps me on the leg bringing me back to the present. "Bug, are you ready?"

"Yeah. I guess." I sigh, slipping off his bike and removing my helmet. I fluff out my hair and tuck my helmet under my arm. I watch as Blayze climbs off his bike. His lean, muscular legs flex with every move. A wanting sensation tingles between my legs from watching him. He smirks as he removes his helmet and places it on the handlebars of his bike. Together we walk into the building.

The dark, dirty hallway always gives me the creeps, but I feel safe with Blayze next to me. I brush off the eerie feeling settling deep in my stomach and continue until we reach the concrete stairs at the end of the hallway. The thump of the bass vibrates through my body as we reach the top of the stairs and head toward my studio at the far end of the hallway. That can only mean John is here early and already producing.

I insert my key and open the door. The bass of the music vibrates the walls. Moans, groans and grunts come from the back of the studio and I quickly walk in that direction. John knows he's not supposed to be directing without me. This shit will end now. He's out of here.

I open the door to the bedroom and it hits the wall with a loud thud. In the middle of the room is a king size bed with crimson sheets and two naked people. There are no cameras or the boom mic set up. John's skinny ass is bare, his hips thrusting into the woman on all fours in front of him. He grunts and groans with every thrust. I can't see who's below him but she's not moving very much, like she's just waiting for this hideous act to be over with. I don't blame her.

I walk over to them and grab John's slicked back hair, yanking him off the bed. He lets out a surprised squeal and hits the ground with a thud. The woman scurries to the other side of the bed, trying to cover herself. Blayze gives her a blanket to cover her body with. I don't pay any attention to her because my focus is on this little fucker messing with my business.

"Who the fuck do you think you are?" I'm seething with anger.

"Monica, what are you doing here?" John looks at me with confusion. He scoots back on the hardwood floor until his back is against the wall and can't go any further. I hope he gets splinters in his ass.

"This is my fucking studio and those are my girls. What in the hell are you doing fucking one of them?" I step next to his skinny body and put my boot on his fingers splayed on the ground. His knuckles crunch under my weight and I smirk. I'm done with the questions.

"Ouch. Stop. Ok, I'll tell you." John howls in pain. I release his hand and he holds it against his chest. "She's not one of the girls. I swear. I'm interviewing her for a scene." John snivels.

"You thought an interview required your pencil dick to do all the talking? Are you fucking kidding me?" I stand above John, waiting for him to make a move. I'll kick this little shit's ass. "In case you couldn't tell, she wasn't enjoying herself at all. Now, get the fuck out of my studio and don't come back. We're done. This partnership I've been forced into with you is over."

John stands up on shaky legs. His limp dick makes me laugh. "What the fuck are you laughing about?" He snarls, trying to intimidate me.

"You. You're a sorry piece of shit. A real man makes sure the woman is enjoying herself. A real man doesn't use his position to stick his dick in a woman. A real man has a bigger dick." I know that last jab will send John over the edge and he doesn't disappoint me.

"You little bitch. You'll wish you never said that." John comes at me fast. He tries to grab my throat but I counteract his move and send my knee into said little dick. He falls to the ground howling in pain. I bring my foot up and connect with his face, sending him on his back. Blood runs down his face and drips onto his chest.

"Get the fuck out now." I squat next to him and yank his hair back so he's looking into my eyes. "You're done in this industry. I'll make sure you never work again." I release his hair and his head hits the floor with a final thud.

John balls up his fist like he's going to hit me. Blayze steps behind me and I rise from my crouched position, standing next to him. "Try it, motherfucker. I've been itching to pull the trigger on your sorry ass." The distinct sound of the safety clicking rings in my ears. John's eyes grow wide with fright and he scurries around to get his clothes.

Once he leaves the studio, I take a seat on the director's chair in the corner and take a few deep breaths. Blayze comes over to me and rests his hands on my knees. "Bug, you OK?"

"Yeah." I clear my throat and straighten my spine. "Yes. I'm good." I look around the room and spot the girl in the corner. She's curled up in a ball against the wall. Her blonde hair is messy and I can't see her face because it's buried in the blanket Blayze gave her. By her appearance, she can't be older than eighteen and that's a strong maybe. "What did she say?"

Blayze follows my stare and his jaw tenses. "That someone named Drew dropped her off for an interview with John. He was supposed to be back to pick her up, but I have a bad feeling about this."

"What do you mean?" I ask.

"I mean, I think I need to call Capone. There's only one Drew I know and he's in our rival Club Blood Scorpions. If he's behind this, then some bad shit's about to go down. Something else is going on. Just look at her." He motions to the girl huddled in the corner. "Why would someone so young come willingly into a strange place like this?"

"Unless this Drew forced her." I finish. "Or she has a bad home life. How about she's on the streets and is looking for work?" I'm grasping at straws here trying to figure this out.

"But let that weasel dick fuck her? Nah, I don't buy it. My gut is telling me something else is going on. I'll be back." Blayze leans over my chair, caging me in with his strong arms. Our lips are a breath apart. "Remember me while I'm gone." He kisses me hard and the butterflies in my stomach flutter around like crazy. Blayze breaks the kiss and I'm panting for air.

"I can never forget you." I breathlessly whisper against his lips.

"Good. I'll be back in a few. See if you can find anything out from her that I couldn't." He leans in and softly kisses my lips. I try to take more, but Blayze pulls away. I pout and he smirks. "Later, Bug."

I watch his fine ass walk out the door, dialing Capone. I release a deep sigh, ogling his lean body. That man is perfect. Movement from the corner catches my attention and I quickly snap out of my lust-filled haze. The girl picks her head up and tears are running down her face. She looks scared and confused. I slowly walk over to her and slide down the wall next to her. She flinches but I brush it away.

"Hey, my name's Monica. What's yours?" I say watching her. She looks around the room like a scared little kitten. She says nothing but when her gaze lands on me, my heart breaks. She didn't want to be here. I can see it in her hazel eyes. "I know you're scared. But trust me, I won't hurt you. I promise."

She wipes the tears from her face. Bruising around her wrist catches my attention. She tucks her hand back inside the blanket before I can stop her. "He's going to kill me for getting caught." Her voice is tiny and afraid.

"Who's going to kill you?" I gently ask.

"I can't say anymore," she whispers, staring off into space.

"Hun, you're safe with me and Xander." I put my hand up and gently rest it on her blanket covered shoulder. "I won't let anyone hurt you anymore, but I need to know what happened."

"You can't protect me." She shakes her head back and forth. "Once he finds out what happened, he'll kill me. I wasn't supposed to get caught."

"Who?" I ask. I don't raise my voice like I want to. This girl has been subjected to too much already in her young life.

"Drew. He left me with that guy. Said it was an interview and if I passed, then I can bring in money for them. Told him to sample the goods and he'd be back for me. Now he's going to kill me." She sobs uncontrollably.

I gather her into my arms and she comes willingly. I soothe her messy hair and comfort her the best I can. "It's OK. I promise. I won't let them hurt you anymore." I say repeatedly, rocking her. "Let's get you dressed. Where are your clothes?" She's still crying but points to the pile of clothes next to the bed. "Come on, let's get you a shower."

I help her up and gather her clothes. Taking one look at them, there's no way I'm letting her put these filthy things back on. "I've got different clothes here. I'm not letting you put these back on. OK?" She nods her head, keeps the blanket wrapped tight around her and I help her into the bathroom. I turn on the shower and let the steam fill the room. "I'll be back in a few. Remember, you're safe here. I won't let anyone get to you. I promise."

"Daisy."

"What's that?"

"My name. It's Daisy. Like the flower." She gives me a small smile.

"It's nice to meet you, Daisy, like the flower. I'll be back in a few minutes." I exit the bathroom, close the door behind me and lean against it. I hear the lock clicking in place.

Tears form in my eyes. Xander was right. Something else is going on and she's the key to figuring out what it is.

Chapter 5

Monica

I head out into the living room, looking for my sexy biker when there's a knock on the door. It's actually more like a boom than a knock making me jump. Xander comes out of the kitchen, tucks his phone into his pocket and answers it. There's a huge burly man wearing a Royal Bastards MC cut standing on the other side. Xander bro hugs him, slapping each other on the back and lets him inside.

"Monica," Xander demands. I step forward toward him. "This is F.O.C.U.S. from our New York City Chapter. F.O.C.U.S., this is my girl, Monica."

"Nice to meet you," I respond, extending my hand. His big burly hand covers mine and gives it a firm shake.

"Same here. Blayze, we have club business to discuss." F.O.C.U.S. says. His deep voice sends a shiver down my spine. I imagine with that timbre and those muscles and tattoos, he can make anyone shiver, male or female.

"You can use my office. It's free from bugs. I do a sweep once a day. Feel free to check again though." I gesture to the closed door behind the kitchen. I give Xander my key.

"Thanks," F.O.C.U.S. responds. He grabs the key out of Xander's fingers and heads to the closed door.

"Everything going OK with the girl?" Xander asks, leaning close. His voice is hushed.

"Yes. I have her in the shower and I'm getting her a fresh change of clothes. I'm afraid you're right though. Something is going on Blayze. We need to protect her." I hold back the anger brewing behind the tears.

"Capone will be here in about twenty minutes. Then we will go over what we know and where to go from there. Just keep an eye on her and keep her safe." He gives me a small kiss and heads into my office with F.O.C.U.S.

I walk into the bedroom that's mine only. When I came back to L.A. to run the porn business, I requested that the studio had a separate bedroom for me. That way I can stay here when I need to and don't have to worry about walking in on anyone. This is my sanctuary.

I cross the hardwood floor and open the top drawer of my dresser. Inside is a wooden box that I keep important information in. I pull out the box and sit on the edge of the bed. With another key, I unlock it. I reach inside and take out the photo that's seen better days. It's a picture of me, Capone, Blayze and Blayze's little sister Danyella taken six months ago. She's a female version of Blayze, with long blonde hair and delicate features. Danyella was a looker and didn't have a mean bone in her body. She kept us all grounded and sane. We were at the clubhouse, smiling like nothing was happening. But after everything I've been through, staring at the picture now, I can see the pain in Danyella's eyes. A few days after this was taken, she disappeared. No word. No trace. She just vanished. It's always haunted Blayze. He's turned this city upside down looking for her but everyone he's talked to knows nothing about her disappearance.

I tuck the picture safely back into the box and put the box back into the dresser. I gather Daisy some clothes and leave my room. I lock the door behind me and head into the studio room. The shower is still on so I clean up the mess John made. I don't want Daisy to see this mess and trigger something. I strip the sheets off the bed and put them in the washer. I grab a new set from the closet and put them on. I clean up the blood off the wall from when I broke John's nose.

When I'm finally finished and everything is back in place, I hear the bathroom door open. Daisy is standing there with a towel wrapped around her body and one wrapped around her hair.

"I didn't see the clothes?" She questions. Her voice is small and timid.

"The door was locked and I didn't want to scare you," I answer. I point to the pile of clothes on my director's chair next to the door. "They're right there. I hope they fit."

"Thank you. I'm sure they'll be better than what I had." Daisy picks up the clothes and heads back into the bathroom. She stops before closing the door. "Thank you for helping me, Monica. I hope I don't bring any trouble to you. These men are dangerous." Tears form in her eyes.

"That's what we're going to figure out. My brother will be here in a few minutes and he will want to talk to you."

"OK. I don't know how much help I'll be but I can try." Daisy closes the door behind her.

A loud bang on the front door startles me. I hurry into the foyer, peek through the peephole and see Capone, Bear, Tiny, and Red waiting on the other side. I unlock the door and allow them inside.

"What's going on?" Capone asks. "I got a call from Blayze telling me about weasel dick fucking some chick."

I roll my eyes with his remark. "Well, he gave you the watered-down version." I gesture to the open living room. I sit in the leather chair. Capone sits on the couch and the rest of the brothers stand around us. "Her name is Daisy and I think she's been kidnapped."

"How'd you come up with that?" Capone asks, resting his elbows on his knees.

"Her dirty clothes, the bruising on her wrists and the way she jumps at everything. She said that some man named Drew left her here and told John he was sampling the goods. He told her that this was an interview. If she fits, then he'd be back to get her."

"And if she didn't?"

"I don't know. What the hell is John doing with my studio?" I stand up and pace back and forth across the floor. "Is he using it for his own sick pleasures or is there something more?" I throw my hands up in the air in frustration.

"Where is John?" Capone's jaw is ticking. He hates it when a woman is hurt. That's his kryptonite.

"I kicked his ass and he ran out of here like a little bitch," I smirk. "After I broke his nose."

"Bear, look into where John went and what he's up to." Capone orders.

"On it, Prez." Bear pulls out his phone and steps out into the hallway.

"Where is the girl now?" Capone asks me.

"She's in the studio bedroom." Capone stands up and heads toward the room. Tiny and Red start to follow him, but they'll scare the fuck out of her. "You two need to stay here. She's already scared and if you go in there, she's going to freak out."

"Stay here and see if you can find a connection to this Drew and John. Then when Blayze comes out of his meeting with F.O.C.U.S., fill him in on what you find." Capone orders.

"You got it, Prez." Red answers.

"My laptop is in the kitchen if you need it guys. Thank you for your help." I offer.

"Anything for Blayze's Bug." Tiny answers with a laugh. He knows that shit bugs the piss out of me. But I guess I'll have to start getting used to it now. I no longer have just an association by blood, but now I'm an unofficial Ol' Lady.

"Smart ass. You're lucky I love you like a brother or I'd kick your ass too." Tiny chuckles. The deep timbre of his laugh makes me smile. Kicking his ass would be like kicking a horse. The man is huge. His arms are bigger than my thighs and he stands well over six foot five. He got his road name Tiny because he's always bringing in tiny stray animals and caring for them.

"Monica? Are we doing this?" Capone snaps.

I roll my eyes and lead him into the bedroom. He's a pissy ass today. Daisy is sitting on the edge of the bed. She looks up when we enter, her hazel eyes are brimmed with tears. I hurry over to her and put my arm around her shoulders. She silently cries into my chest and I soothe her the best I can. Capone crosses the room and takes a seat in my director's chair.

"Daisy, this is Capone, my brother and the President of Royal Bastards MC. He's going to help us in figuring out what's going on." My voice is soft and gentle.

Daisy raises her head and looks at Capone. Her breath catches in her throat and her body trembles with fear. "No. This can't be happening." She's on the verge of a breakdown.

"What's wrong?" I'm trying my best to keep her with me, but she's spiraling.

"No. No. No. You're with Royal Bastards? Oh, man. They're really going to kill me." She shakes her head back and forth. "I've got to get out of here."

"Yes, we are. But I won't let anyone kill you. You're safe with us." Capone's voice is gentle even though I can see the tick in his jaw.

"You don't understand. The last girl that was involved with the Royal Bastards disappeared and I never saw her again." Daisy sobs. "She was my best friend in there. We had each other's backs, but she just vanished."

Capone and I stare at each other. My eyes are wide and my jaw drops. There has only been one girl who's disappeared from the RBMC and never seen again.

Danyella.

Chapter 6

Blayze

I'm out of my meeting with F.O.C.U.S. from the Royal Bastards New York City Chapter. That man is intense. Every time he leaves, I feel like I need a long nap to recharge. He left with the rest of his brothers, heading back to their Chapter. I'm walking toward the studio bedroom, searching for Monica when I hear a pissed off grumble behind me. Turning around, I spot Tiny sitting in the leather chair with Monica's laptop resting on his big knees. He's rubbing his stubbled jaw with one hand and his eyebrows are furrowed with concentration. Red is standing behind him with the same expression.

"Tiny, Red? What's up?" I ask, halting my steps toward the studio bedroom. I turn and head back to where they're at.

Tiny looks up from the laptop. His normal California tanned face is pale but his brown eyes are screaming violence. "Prez has us looking into the connection to John and the fucker named Drew. Bear is searching John's most recent whereabouts after he left here."

"What'd you find?"

"Prez told me about your hunch and it was right. I found video surveillance of Drew dropping that little girl off with John. The same fucker that's a part of Bloody Scorpions, our biggest rival. They're asshole deep into human trafficking and VP, you're not going to like what I've found. There's a list of girls on the black market for sale." Tiny continues before I lose my shit and force it out of him. "I created an account to enter their auction." He turns the laptop toward me and my breath catches in my throat. There are over thirty girls ranging from the age of thirteen to twenty on the screen.

"What the fuck is this?" I ask aloud. It's a rhetorical question. I'm shocked and pissed.

"That's not the worst part, Blayze." Tiny clicks a tab and another image fills the screen. One I know immediately. Danyella, my baby sister who's been missing for six months.

My ears ring and rage boils my blood looking at my little sister's image. She's scared and confused. The once vibrant smile and sparkle in her familiar green eyes are gone. I'm going to tear apart the Bloody Scorpions and rip each member limb from limb. I will rip their dicks off and shove them up their asses for fucking with my family. Their blood will be on my hands and I'll enjoy every minute of it.

"Blayze?" I hear Monica, but her sweet gentle voice is so far away. "Blayze!" Monica shouts.

I look in the direction her voice came from, but I'm so blinded by rage, I don't actually see her. I'm looking past her. Clicking boots on the hardwood flooring and small, warm hands rub my arms. Monica's voice breaks through the ringing in my ears. I turn my head; tears are in my eyes. Monica opens her arms and I go into them. She runs her hands through my hair, soothing my tortured soul. Trying to bring me back to reality.

"Shh. It'll be OK, Blayze. We'll figure out a way to get her back. I promise you." Monica's voice cracks. This is hard for all of us. Danyella and Monica were as close as sisters. I need to pull my shit together and go at this with a level head. I straighten my spine and look around the room. Capone, Bear, Red, Tiny and the girl are watching me, waiting for me to go on a rampage. The girl looks scared as fuck. Does she have any information?

"She doesn't," Monica answers my unspoken question. She sighs, "I know your train of thought, Blayze. Daisy doesn't know where Danyella is. The only thing she knows is one day they were together and the next, she was gone. She hasn't seen Danyella in almost a week."

"A week? She's been missing for six fucking months!" I try to rein in the anger in my voice, but it's useless.

Monica doesn't even bat an eye at my outburst. Daisy jumps. "I know. But let's look at it this way. She went missing six months ago, but Daisy saw her a week ago. They've been inseparable for the last five months." Monica rests her palms on my face, making me hear her. "She has been with Danyella for five months. We finally have a lead. And to top it off, we know ass fuck and some dick named Drew are working together. Once we find their connection, we can move forward."

"Blayze, we need to take this to the table. Church in an hour." Capone speaks up for the first time since I found this information out. Capone and Danyella were close too. She has that way about her where everyone gravitates toward her.

"Be right behind you, Prez." I nod my head. "I just need a minute to wrap my head around this."

"I'll stay with him, Capone. Can you take Daisy to the clubhouse? Put her in my room and keep her safe, please." I put my arm around Monica's shoulders. She doesn't leave my side. I'm so thankful for that.

"Consider it done. Bear, Daisy can ride with you." Capone orders. Daisy's trembling again from head to toe. Monica leaves the warmth of my arm and walks to her. They say something back and forth and finally Daisy nods her head and wipes the tears away. She straightens her spine and follows my brothers out of the studio. They keep her between them all, protecting her.

Once the door closes behind them, Monica turns her face upward toward me. Her gentle brown eyes are full of compassion. "I'm so sorry, Xander. I was hoping this wasn't true, but it is. Now, we need to get to the club and make a plan. We can't go in there half-cocked and get Danyella and possibly ourselves killed."

"I know, Bug. I know. I'm so pissed thinking she's been here hidden from me for the past six months. Someone out there knows something." I grind my teeth to stop myself from flying off the handle.

"And we will figure out who." Monica places her hands on my cheeks, keeping me grounded. "Once we find her, you'll have free rein to do what you do; inflict as much pain and suffering on them as you can."

"I love the way your mind works." I lean down, closing the space between our lips. I wrap an arm around Monica's waist and pull her against me. Her soft curves ignite an inferno throughout my body. I kiss and nip up the column of her throat. I need to forget for just a little while. I need her body to help erase the image of my baby sister being held captive. I need to be grounded and this woman is the only one who can control my tortured soul.

"Do it, Xander. Take my body the way you need it." The lust dripping from her voice fuels me on.

I pick Monica up so she can wrap her legs around my waist and carry her toward her bedroom. Her lips are everywhere, peppering my face, ears and throat with kisses.

"Unlock the door." My voice is husky with need.

Monica pulls her lips off my neck and I set her feet on the floor. She turns around and I keep her against me, trailing my hands underneath her t-shirt, cupping her breasts. They fill my hands perfectly. She squirms under my grasp, but I don't stop. I lick and suck the side of her neck, driving her insane. If she doesn't unlock her door in three seconds, I will take her against the wall.

Monica fumbles with the keys to unlock her door, but she finally gets it. Once the door swings open, I lead us into the bedroom. She's still in front of me with her back against my chest. I yank her t-shirt up over her head and dump it on the floor. Monica unbuttons her jeans.

"Fuck, Xander." Monica pants. She bucks her hips into my hand. She's ready for me. Monica brings an arm up behind us and grips the back of my head, running her fingernails through my hair. I continue to tease her with my fingers and kiss the side of her neck. She's panting, moaning and gripping my hair with force.

I remove my hand and yank her jeans down her legs. She steps out of them and turns toward me. Removing my cut, she carefully places it on the dresser. It's a huge turn on, Monica respecting the cut and patch. By the time she comes back to me, I've already removed my T-shirt and jeans. Monica stands in front of me and drops to her knees. She pulls my boxers down and my erection springs free from its confinement. I kiss her hard.

Monica breaks the kiss and crawls onto her bed. She looks at me over her shoulder from all fours, her ass teasing me.

Monica wiggles her hips, trying to slide down onto me. I grip her hip with one hand to stop her from succeeding.

Monica arches her back and I lean over her, trailing kisses up her spine. I wrap one hand around her waist and pull her up until she's straddling me. We're both sweating from the passion flowing through our bodies. She's so close, I can feel it and smell it in the air. I can taste it on her skin.

"Fuck, you are the most precious thing," I growl against her heaving chest.

Tingles start at the base of my spine and fire races through my veins. Sensations burn through my body.

"Come for me, Monica. Now." I demand. She meets my lips with her own and her core tightens even more. Monica's orgasm takes over her body and she loudly shouts my name. I'm a goner. Fire shoots up my spine.

It's not enough. Now I have to take her the way I need it, hard and fast. Monica doesn't complain. Fire races through my spine and I know I'm close. She moans and arches her back, drawing me into her deeper. A few more thrusts and I'm thrown over the edge of bliss, wrapped around my Ol' Lady.

By the time I catch my breath, Monica is fully sated underneath me, and I feel like I'm the king of the fucking universe with the flush of her cheeks and the rapid rise and fall of her chest. I roll off to the side, pulling her with me.

"Hmm..." she purrs against my neck.

"With as much as I want to stay here, we can't. I have to get to the clubhouse before your brother maims me for being late." I kiss the top of Monica's forehead and she lets out a breath.

"Fine, But I'm not responsible if I fall asleep on the ride over and tumble to my death on the back of your bike. You wore me out." She huffs with fake annoyance. I can't help but release a deep chuckle.

"Get dressed and let's roll, sweet cheeks." I wink and swing my legs over the bed. I'm in the bathroom before Monica can retaliate. She hates being called nicknames like that and I enjoy doing it just to see the spark of fire in her eyes.

"You're such an ass," Monica mumbles from the other side of the door. I relieve myself, wash my hands and take a long look in the mirror. My eyes portray the rage pouring inside my soul. I have unfinished business with John James and the Bloody Scorpions. They fucked with the wrong badass motherfucker. Blood and pain will be inflicted on them and when I'm done, they'll wish their faces never came through the cunt of their mother.

"I'm coming for you."

Chapter 7

Blayze

The ride back to Royal Bastards Clubhouse was uneventful. Monica didn't fall off the back of my bike like she thought, but she sure as fuck played with my erection the whole way. Which took my mind off the shit my sister has been through. Riding with a boner is hard, literally.

I pull up outside the gates, the sun beating down onto us and wait for Tiny and a prospect to let us in. They spot my bike and the gates buzz before rolling open on the track. I ease my bike inside and the buzzer sounds again, closing the gates behind me. I roll past the parking lot toward the garage bays when one lifts open. I idle inside and park my bike in my designated spot. Capone, Bear, Red, Dagger, Derange, Tiny and Trigger are already here, their bikes parked in their designated spots.

I cut the engine, put my kickstand down and tap Monica on the leg. She rests one hand on my shoulder. She swings her leg off the bike and dismounts with grace. I watch as she removes the helmet she hates wearing and fluffs out her hair. She turns to me with a knowing grin on her face.

"Ready?" She asks, tucking her helmet under her arm.

I shake my head and dismount, adjusting my dick and willing it to go down. The last thing I need is to walk into Church with seven other men sporting a hard-on. I unclip my helmet and set it on the handlebar of my bike. Pocketing my keys, I settle an arm around Monica's shoulder and breathe in her scent. She smells like jasmine, sex and me. That's not helping my situation. We walk together down the corridor into the common room, the click of our riding boots echoing through the hall. Club bunnies dance to the beat of the music drifting from the speakers. Monica stiffens under my arm and I sneak a glance at her.

"Bug, what's wrong?"

"Nothing." She shakes her head.

I look to where her eyes are and spot Samantha sitting at the bar nursing a beer. She turns her head toward us and there are fresh bruises on her face. My stomach sinks. Samantha gives us a sneer and slides off the stool. She approaches us on unsteady feet. Monica stands with her feet shoulder-width apart. I can feel the rage vibrating through her body the closer Samantha gets.

"I hope you're happy with yourself." Samantha slurs, throwing her hands up. She points to her face. "This...This is all your fault, you high and mighty bitch."

"How in the fuck is that my fault?" Monica challenges.

Samantha chuckles. "Because if it wasn't for you, the other Ol' Ladies wouldn't have jumped me." She steps right up into Monica's face. I can smell the liquor and weed on her breath. "Watch your back you little bitch. I'm coming for you."

"Back off before I put my foot up your ass." Monica shrugs my arm off her shoulder. "You want a run at me? Come on. Sober up and fight me, then." She steps forward, making Samantha step back. "You want to blame me for fucking shit up? Then, let's go. You," Monica points a finger in Samantha's face. "You're a used-up has-been who can't get a man, let alone keep one. You want to come at me?" She steps again and Samantha scurries back. "Then come at me, bitch. I'll be here with my man all night long. And guess what? While he's fucking me, he sure in the fuck isn't thinking about you. He never has and never will."

Monica's body is trembling with rage when Capone steps out of the hallway. He watches with narrowed eyes waiting to see what Samantha does. Samantha opens her mouth to say something but quickly snaps it shut when her eyes land on the club members backing up Monica. From the bunnies to the Ol' Ladies (which are few and far between) to my brothers. They all have Monica's back and pride swells in my chest. I step up behind Monica and rest my hands on her shoulders.

"I'll give you one more chance to be smart, Samantha." Capone's deep voice penetrates the tension in the air. "You can either make an ass of yourself now and get kicked out for good or get the fuck in your room and don't come out until you've settled down and sobered up."

Samantha looks at Capone and her shoulders fall. I know she's had a thing for him since the beginning but he's smarter than she thinks and sees her for what she really is. The club bitch. She's good at her job in keeping others in line, but she sucks at staying in line herself. Samantha turns on her heels and walks quickly out of the common room grumbling under her breath. Once she's out of sight, Capone heads toward us.

"Church, now." He turns toward the Chapel and stops before he enters. "Daisy is in your room like you asked. Jezebelle is in there with her and a prospect is guarding the door."

"Thank you, Capone." Capone nods his head once and walks into Church. The rest of the main members follow, leaving us alone.

"I'll see you in a little while. Please, don't leave your room until I come and get you." I plead with Monica.

"Ok, but only because you asked nicely. I'm heading there now." She gives me a quick kiss and disappears in the direction of her room.

Once she's out of sight, I head into Church. I'm the last one in and close the door behind me. I take my respective seat to the left of Capone who's at the head of the table. Every time I come in and take my seat, I cross my chest and kiss my fingers, a superstition I have and do before each meeting.

"Now, we have business to discuss." Capone starts, banging his gavel on the oak table. Our Royal Bastards MC logo is etched deep into the wood with nicks and marks around it. This table has seen better days but also holds a sense of pride to each and every one of us sitting around it. It's heard our confessions, held our tears and comforted each of us when we needed it. Now, it's my turn.

I steeple my hands together in front of me and release a deep breath I didn't realize I was holding. "We found out some info today that changes a lot of things for me." I glance up, looking at each brother sitting at the table. Bear, Red, Tiny, Trigger, Derange, Torch and Dagger are all watching me, waiting for what I have to say next.

"Danyella," I swallow hard and continue. "Danyella is still alive." Gasps explode into the quiet room along with everyone talking above each other.

Capone slams the gavel on the table, silencing the room. "He's not done. Now bite your fucking tongues until Blayze is finished."

"We discovered today that she's being held captive by Bloody Scorpions and is scheduled to go up for auction tonight. Tiny has set up an account and will be placing the bid on her to get her back. If that goes through and we win, we need to have a plan to get her out. Then, we need to find where these fuckers are holding the rest of the girls and end them." I slam my fist on the table, making it vibrate.

"How many girls and how much money?" Trigger asks. He's the Treasurer of our Chapter and keeps track of all the finances.

"The bidding starts at ten grand," Tiny answers. "From the looks of their website, they have five girls up tonight, but I'm guessing they have around twenty, maybe more."

"How did we not know all these women are missing?" This comes from Dagger our Chaplin, sitting at the end of the table. He runs his hands down his face and over his black goatee.

"Because they're not all from this area. These guys are smart and kidnap women and girls from different states and transport them here." Red answers. He's strumming his fingers on the table, itching to seek revenge. "I ran a check on a few of them through a missing persons report when I got back here and had the adequate tools to work with. One woman on the block tonight is from Michigan." He levels both Capone and me with a stare. "Central Michigan to be exact."

My jaw drops open. Capone sucks in a deep breath. We know what that means and neither one of us has really thought about Savage Saints since they left here.

But it looks like we need to make a phone call soon. I look at Capone who's ticking his jaw. The only sign he's pissed off. His black eyes swing in my direction and nods his head. That phone call is coming sooner, rather than later.

"What's the rest of the plan?" Bear asks. His burly arms cross over his chest and he leans back in his chair, creaking under his weight.

"We go in, get Danyella out and fuck shit up." Torch, our Enforcer responds. He got his nickname Torch because after he's finished with an enemy, he lights their body on fire and he enjoys the torture that comes with it.

"It has to be more than that. We need to make sure these fuckers are brought down for good. If we have to take out their whole club, that's what we'll do." Capone growls from his seat. "These motherfuckers need to be stopped for good. Tiny, get on their site and be ready for a bidding war. Trigger, Torch and Red, once we get a location where Bloody Scorpions are holding the girls, your job will be to get to their clubhouse and set up around their perimeter. No one in, no one out. Blayze, Derange, Bear and I will be at the girls' location to get them out. I'll have a prospect waiting with the van to escort the girls back here. Then, once they're safely out, we hit Bloody Scorpions MC with everything we have. No mercy." Capone slams his gavel down on the table, ending our meeting.

Tiny is the first to get up and leave Church. There's a haunting look in his eyes and I know that expression well. This is hard on him. I'll have to check on him before we leave. Trigger, Torch and Red walk out together next, talking about where they'll set up and how they'll keep Bloody Scorpions in the clubhouse. That leaves us with Bear and Derange.

Derange leans forward and sets his hands on the table, running his fingers over the scarred wood. He looks up, "What's this mean for us? Bloody Scorpions are huge. There's no way we can take them on our own."

"I'll call in reinforcements. Get some allies on our side. Be prepared for a blood bath, brother." There's a hint of revenge in his voice. He wants blood, just like the rest of us.

Dagger stands up from his seat and exits Church without another word. "I'll go check on him. Make sure he's in the right frame of mind for this. Something has been going on with Jezebelle." Bear stands up and follows Dagger out. That leaves Capone and me.

Capone pulls his phone out of his jeans and sets it on the table. "Better make that phone call now. Get them ready." He punches a button and puts it on speaker phone.

It rings several times before a sultry voice answers. "This better be good."

"It is. I have some information that we need your help on." Capone responds.

"I'm listening."

"We have a location on some missing girls and a few of them are from Central Michigan. I know you have connections out there." This is hard admitting we need help. I can see it in the way Capone swallows hard.

"I do. But what does that have to do with me? You've made it clear you never wanted nor needed our help." She's not giving Capone an inch.

"I was wrong, Krimson. We need your help. I need your crew to help us get Blayze's sister back." Capone pleads with her. Krimson is the leader of the street racers in Los Angeles. She took down the biggest motherfucker of them all a couple of years ago after she found out he killed her parents and kidnapped her little brother.

"You've found Danyella? Why in the fuck didn't you lead with that?" I hear her inhale a deep breath through the phone. "What's the plan?"

"Bloody Scorpions are having an auction tonight. Tiny is set up to bid on her and is searching for where they might be holding the girls. It looks like they have about five up for auction. A total of twenty or more girls waiting. That's a lot of bodies to be moving at one time. Once we have the location, three of my men will be set up outside their clubhouse. Then me, Bear, Derange and Blayze will be at the girls' location, ready to get them out. We will end them tonight. I need a safe passage through the city for our van to get back here." Capone exhales and rubs his temples.

"Anything else?" Krimson asks.

"We need help taking these motherfuckers out. They're a big MC and we don't have the manpower. My other Chapters are too far away to make it here." Krimson doesn't answer. She's waiting to hear the words flow through my Prez's lips. He knows it too because he clenches his fists on the table. "Krimson, will your crew help us destroy these trafficking motherfuckers?"

Silence from the other end of the phone is making my blood boil. I open my mouth to tell her never mind and to fuck off when Capone raises his hand silencing me.

"Yes, you'll have my help. I'll arrange a safe passage through the city. Once you figure out the route back to your clubhouse, let me know and I'll have the streets shut down. Rush, Hotflash, Redlight, Quickshift, Nolan and his men, along with myself will assist you in ending these motherfuckers. They messed with the wrong woman. Bringing that shit into my city is unacceptable. Be ready to shed some blood, boys." Krimson hangs up before Capone or I can say anything.

"That went better than I expected," Capone leans back in his seat. He stares off into space before turning in my direction. "Is it me or does that woman cause a shiver down your spine?"

"Oh, she scares the shit out of me. If there's one woman besides mine that I don't want to cross," I point to the phone like she can see me, "It's her."

Capone laughs and slaps the table. "Alright, brother. Let's go check on the rest of the guys and see what they've come up with."

We exit Church and head for the communications room. Tiny is in there along with Red. They're both at different computers, searching for shit. Tiny has photos up of different missing girls. He has them labeled and marked by state. Red is searching for traffic cameras in different parts of the city. They have shit under control and I turn to leave.

"Hey, Prez. VP." Red calls out, halting my steps. "I found something and you're not going to like it."

I turn back around and step behind Red, looking at the screen he has up. Capone stands next to me. "What'd you find?"

Red hits play and the screen comes to life. It's grainy but I can make out a man walking with two girls. One can't be older than four. She's clutching onto the other woman like her life depends on the woman's survival. I can't make out who the woman is. Her head is down and her snarly hair is covering her face. The man yanks on the woman's hair hard. She lets out a squeal of protest but remains upright. He has on a leather cut but I can't make out the patches from this angle. The man shouts in the woman's face, getting right in her personal space. The woman turns to face the camera and my heart stops beating.

    Danyella.

She stares directly at me and mouths something into the camera before he yanks on her hair again, pulling her and the little girl down an alley and out of sight.

"Rewind that. Where are they?" I order Red. I stare at the screen again, trying to make out what she's saying. "What the fuck is she telling me?" Red hits play again and I watch Danyella's mouth move.

"They're at the corner of West 5th and South Hill Street, in downtown L.A. There's construction going on in that area. Perfect place to move a bunch of women and citizens wouldn't even know. With all the trucks going in and out, it'd be a breeze to add one more to the mix. I'll bet my patch that's where they are. I'll keep looking to see if anyone else goes in and out of that area. Then, I'll try to figure out what Danyella is trying to say." Red answers.

"Good work brother." Capone slaps his back.

"Yeah, good work." I echo Capone. I need to get out of here. I need air. My shirt is strangling my neck. Sweat beading on my brow. I head for the door and get out of that room as fast as I can. Worry and dread fill my stomach thinking about everything Danyella has gone through the past six months. I walk down the hallway to Monica's room as quickly as my boots will take me. If one person can ground me when I need it, it's her.

Chapter 8

Monica

My bedroom door slams open with a hard thud. Daisy jumps from her seated position on my bed and scurries to the attached bathroom. Her blue eyes turn wide and her body starts shaking in fear. Blayze is on the other side of the door. His chest is heaving and sweat beading on his brow. My room grows smaller with the tension radiating from his body. His green eyes are haunted, portraying the pain he's in. He searches the room and that deadly gaze lands on me. I've seen him like this only once before and that was when Steam and Chains tried to kill me.

I approach Blayze cautiously, "Xander, what's wrong?" His body relaxes a little when I approach him and he wraps his muscular arms around my shoulders, drawing me into him. He holds on tight, not letting go. "Xander, talk to me, please."

"We found her. We found Danyella." I should be relieved but I know better. Being in this life you learn how to take the good with the bad.

"But…" I trail off waiting for him to finish.

"But she's being held by Bloody Scorpions in a construction area in downtown L.A. We can't get to her." His voice chokes on the last part. "I've failed her like I've failed you." Blayze buries his face in my hair and breathes deep.

"Xander, you didn't fail me. What happened to me has nothing to do with you." I comfort him, wrapping my arms around his waist. "You didn't do that to me. Steam and Chains did."

"But if it wasn't for me sending you there, you would've never been in their crosshairs." Blayze counters.

"If I stayed here, Chains would've killed me to prove a point to Capone. What happened to me isn't your fault." I cup his face, making him look at me. "You saved me. You sacrificed your patch to keep me alive and I'm still here. I'm not six feet under. I have air in my lungs and you by my side. That's all I need and all I want." Blayze buries his face in my hair again, pulling me closer to him.

Daisy approaches us. I forgot she was in the room, "I know how to get in. If you take me there, I can help." The meek little girl I found crumpled on the floor of my studio wants to help.

Blayze lifts his face from my hair and pins Daisy with a glare. She shrinks back a little. "No. Absolutely not. You're not going back there." His arms tighten around my shoulders.

"It was just an idea," Daisy fidgets with the hem of her t-shirt. She casts her gaze to the carpet.

"I won't have you in any more danger. You're safe here inside our clubhouse." Blayze looks at me. "I have to leave. I want you to promise me that you'll stay inside and won't leave."

I don't answer right away. "God fucking damn it, Monica. Stay here so I don't have to worry about you while I'm trying to get my sister back." Blayze's voice is deadly.

"Fine. But if you're not back, I'm coming for you. If you die trying to rescue Danyella, I will bring you back to life just to kill you all over again." I'm serious too.

"I'll be safe. I promise. But you know it's a chance every time I step out that door."

"I know, Xander. I know."

Blayze leans down until our lips are a hairsbreadth apart. His green eyes are boring right into me. Into my soul. Our lips crash together. He runs his tongue along the seam and I open. His tongue plunges inside my mouth, stealing my breath and the rest of my heart along with it. Blayze pulls away and rests his forehead against mine.

"I love you, Xander," I breathe into him, clutching his leather cut with both hands.

"I love you too, Monica. Until my last breath."

I inhale a sharp breath and tears form in my eyes. Blayze gently wipes them away with the pad of his thumbs. He gathers me into his arms again and kisses the side of my neck, sending heat to my core.

"Blayze, time to roll, now." Capone stands in the middle of my door, taking up the whole space. His body is vibrating with revenge. There's a slight tick in his jaw. The only telltale sign he's pissed. His black eyes land on me and he gives me a small nod. We might be half-siblings, but we're in sync with each other. He knows I'll worry about them all until they come back safe.

"Bring our family home." I plead with Capone.

"Always." He turns on his heels and leaves, taking the tension with him.

"I'll see you soon, Bug. And when I do, you better be ready for me." Blayze kisses me one last time before he walks out of my room, taking my heart with him.

I don't know how long I stand in the doorway, my heart hurting for my family right now. All I can do is wait, but that's not one of my strong points. I have to do something. I turn to Daisy, "Come on, I need a drink."

We walk to the bar. It's too quiet out here. No music pumping from the speakers. No club bunnies milling around, looking for a dick to fall on. All the club members but a few prospects and lower-ranking patch members are on the rescue mission.

I stroll behind the bar and point to a stool on the other side. Daisy sits down and watches me work. I hand her a bottled water and fix myself a drink. She uncaps the water and drinks like she hasn't had anything this refreshing in a long time. I sip my drink slowly, looking around the common room. No one is paying us any attention, which will work with what's going on in my head. My eyes land on Daisy when she finishes her water.

"What?" She asks.

"You know how to get in the building?"

"Yes..." Daisy trails off. She's scared and I don't blame her. What I'm going to ask her to do next will put us both in danger but fuck it. I'm not waiting any longer.

"I have a plan but I need your help executing it." She nods her head, waiting for me to continue. "We're going on a field trip of sorts."

"But Blayze told you to stay here."

"Yeah, I know." I wave my hand dismissively. "But Daisy, I can't just stay here and let my family go head first into danger. There's one thing you should know about me. I don't follow directions or orders very well."

"I'm figuring that out. What can I do?" She crushes her water bottle and I throw it away.

"I'm going to head into that room." I point to the communications room. "You're going to be my lookout. If someone comes, you give me a warning. There shouldn't be a problem since most of the guys are gone. Then, when I find what I need, we're out of here."

"OK."

"That's my girl. Stick with me kid, I'll show you how to get shit done." I knock my knuckles on the bar top. Looking around, I see my chance to get in and out. None of the guys are paying attention to us. I hurry towards the communications room and pick the lock. I look behind me and Daisy is swiveled on her stool so she's watching the whole room. She nods her head at me and I slip inside.

I look around the room. The computers are still on and a screen displays a countdown. Two hours and thirty minutes left until the auction. Above the countdown is a picture of Danyella. Only it doesn't really look like her. Her vibrant green eyes are haunted. Her once shiny straight blonde hair is dirty and scraggly. She has fresh bruises on her face and neck.

"What have they done to you, Danyella?" I touch the screen with my fingertips, tracing her face. A lone tear trails down my cheek and I wipe it away. The red lights ticking down remind me I'm on a time limit. There will be time later to grieve for what she's lost. What we've all lost.

I flick the mouse to the other computer and it fires up, revealing what I'm looking for. There's an older building deep in the heart of downtown Los Angeles. There are photos of the specs of the building. I study them and commit them to memory. An address is written down on a sticky note. I commit that to memory also.

Red is getting sloppy with his work. I will have to talk to Capone about that. He not only left the location of the girls on a sticky note, but he also left the address of Bloody Scorpions' Clubhouse. What if it wasn't me in here? What if someone broke into our clubhouse and discovered all the information, they needed in one glance? This is unacceptable.

I turn to leave when I hear Daisy whistling. She's humming a tune that I've heard before but can't quite place where. I hurry to the door and crack it open. One prospect is facing towards the door, crowding Daisy's space and she's on the verge of a panic attack. She spots me and relief washes over her face. I see her turn her back to the prospect, getting him to move around her. When his back is to me, I slip out the door.

"Come on, baby. You know playing hard to get is a huge turn on." I hear the prospect trying to hit on Daisy. "I can show you a good time if you're game."

"No, I'm good. Thanks anyway." Daisy dismisses the prospect with a wave of her hand. He still isn't giving up though and now I'm getting pissed.

"Oh, don't be like that, baby." He crowds his body into her and she's trying to push him away.

"I said no." Daisy is gasping for breath. Her chest is heaving up and down rapidly.

"No means yes, right?" Doesn't this fucker get the hint?

I sneak up behind him and when he tries to touch Daisy, I grab his hand. I put pressure on the spot between his thumb and pointer finger, yanking his hand behind his back.

"What the fuck!" The prospect squeals.

"I think the lady told you no." I press down harder. Prospect drops to his knees, gritting his teeth. "Now apologize to my friend." He opens his mouth then shuts it again. I squeeze his hand harder. I can feel the bones crunching together under my fingertips. "Now," I growl.

"I'm sorry. There is that good enough." He whines in pain.

I release his hand and shove him forward with my foot. He falls face first and scrambles to get up. Prospect turns around like he's going to do something and I raise an eyebrow with my hands on my hips. "You better think again, prospect. If you want to make it in this club, learn this lesson real quick. No does not mean yes. And if you want to hit a woman, be prepared to have the whole MC on your ass. We don't tolerate that shit here." I turn my attention to Daisy. "You good?"

"Yeah, thanks, Monica." Daisy wraps her arms around her waist, trying to get her shivering under control.

"C'mon, girl. I've got some stuff to do." Daisy rises from the stool but before she follows me, she turns toward the prospect.

"I'm not what you guys call a club bunny. I don't like to be touched. Next time," Daisy reaches into the pocket of her jeans pulling a knife out. Holy shit. Where in the hell did, she get that? Daisy flicks it open and points the blade at the prospect, "Next time, I will cut your balls off and shove them down your throat. I'm sick of you men thinking you can touch me whenever you want. Unless I give the go ahead, don't fucking touch me." With that she turns on her heels, leaving the prospect standing there stunned.

I must have the same expression on my face because Daisy slows her steps down. Her eyes are turning red like she will cry. "Am I in trouble?"

"Hell, the fuck no, girl. I'm surprised."

"It felt good to finally be able to defend myself." She closes the knife with expert precision and puts it back in her front jeans pocket.

"Well now that's out of the way, we need to get out of here." I loop my arm through Daisy's and lead her away from the still stunned prospect.

We walk down the corridor that leads to where the guys park their bikes. I cross over to the shelf and find a set of keys hanging on the hook. I snatch them down and together Daisy and I approach the door that leads out of the garage. I open it and peek outside. The moon shines brightly onto the parking lot and the heat from the day blasts me in the face.

"Quickly, before they realize what we're up to." I push the door open further and make my way to a sleek black Dodge Charger, Daisy right on my heels. I hit the button to unlock the doors and we climb inside. I push the button to fire her up and turn the air conditioner on full blast. I pull out of the parking spot and head right for the gates. No one is out here watching who comes in and out. I park the car, hurry over to the button hidden in the wall and the gates buzz. I hurry back to the car and wait as the gate slowly rolls open. I nudge my way through and park the car. I get out again and push another hidden button on the side of the guard shack. The gates buzz again and roll shut. I peel out leaving tire marks and dust behind me.

"Wow, all that and no one knows we left?" Daisy questions.

"I'm sure someone was alerted. Those gates have a wireless connection to the guys' phones." As soon as the words leave my mouth, my phone lights up with an incoming call. Blayze's name flashes across the screen. He's going to be pissed I left. I swipe the red button sending him to voicemail. My phone lights up again. This time Capone's name flashes across the screen. I hesitate to send him to voicemail. I do it anyways. If they know what we're up to, they'll try to stop us.

"Are you going to get into trouble?" Daisy asks.

"Probably." I shrug my shoulders. My phone lights up again with another incoming call from Blayze. I ignore it and continue to drive. "If they would've let me come along, I wouldn't have to do this behind their backs."

My phone rings again. Blayze. Maybe I should answer it. My finger hesitates over the green answer button but at the last second, I power down my phone. "There. Now they can't call." I'm not stupid enough to remove the battery. If I get into trouble, they'll be able to track me.

"What's the plan?"

"We get to where they're holding Danyella, sneak in, get her out and come back here," I say it as simply as I can.

"It's not going to be that simple. They have guards everywhere."

"That's what you're here for. You know their rotations and when they're busy. You know which guard would rather get his dick wet, even by force than, do his job."

Daisy shudders and closes her eyes. "Yeah, I do. If J.J. is there, then all bets are off. That little fuck had no right to do what he did to me."

"Was that the first time someone forced themselves on you?" I ask as gently as I can.

She nods her head. "Yes. And I want to cut off his balls for taking that power away from me."

"You'll get your chance. I'll make sure of it." I squeeze her hand and put my hands back on the steering wheel.

"Thank you again, Monica," Daisy replies. "I was so scared when Drew dropped me off."

"You're welcome. I'm glad it was me who found you." I give her a small smile. This girl has been through so much in her young life I hope and pray she will find some normalcy when this is over.

Thirty minutes later, I pull up to a building and park the car. "We're here," I state into the quietness of the car. I check the loaded nine-mil and tuck it in the holster. Then I check to make sure the knife is still tucked in my boot and another one at my back. Once I'm satisfied, I look over at Daisy. She's playing with the hem of her t-shirt.

"There's an entrance to the back around that building." Daisy points to the south of the old run-down building. "They kept us in the basement."

I glance at the clock and see we have an hour and a half left until the auction. Time is not on our side as I get out of the car and quietly close the door. Daisy does the same. Together, we creep in the shadows of the building. The city traffic drowns out our footsteps. Daisy's steps falter the closer we get.

"What's wrong?" I ask.

"This is it. This is the back entrance."

I tug on the back door and it's locked. I pull out my lock picking set and get to work. After a few minutes, I hear the distinct click of the tumblers moving, gaining us access. I open the door and wait for an alarm. When nothing happens, I motion for Daisy to go inside.

She shakes her head, her body trembling with fear. "I don't know if I can do this, Monica."

I approach Daisy being careful not to let the door close and rub her arms. "Daisy, you don't have to. I can do this on my own. You have every right to be scared. But this will be your way to gain back the power they took. Trust me, I know about losing that power." My hands instinctively rub my stomach, over the scars Steam and Chains left me with.

"What happened to you?"

I open my mouth to answer and quickly close it. Heavy footsteps coming from the alley approach us at a rapid pace. "We have to hide, c'mon." I tug at Daisy's arm and together we hunker down in the dark stairwell of the abandoned warehouse. I don't let the door slam behind me. A few seconds later, the same door opens and we plaster our bodies against the wall, trying to stay out of sight. As the heavy footsteps come closer, my breathing picks up and my heart is beating hard against my chest. I close my eyes and steady my racing heart, slowing my breath.

"Did you hear something?" A deep timber asks.

"No. What did you hear?" Another man answers. I recognize that voice. He's haunted my dreams for the past year.

I try to look at Daisy in the darkness but I can't see her. I reach out to her and she slowly clutches my hand in a death like grip.

"Must've been rats. I don't hear anything now." The first man says.

"Then get your ass back to your post. Word has it The Royal Bastards snagged one of our girls and beat the shit out of my future son in law." The second man answers.

What in the hell is he talking about? The only person we have is Daisy and they didn't beat anyone up.

"Let me see that fucker they call a V.P. His ass is mine. After the way he humiliated my brother, I will end him." The man with the deep timber says. There's vengeance in his voice.

I'm confused as hell about what they're talking about. I'm wracking my brain trying to figure it out and don't hear them step closer. Daisy's hand squeezes mine harder and her body is trembling. I look to where she's looking and my breath catches in my throat. The first man is staring right in our direction. I don't think he can see us because if he can, we'd be dead or captured. Maybe it wasn't a good idea to come here without backup. He cocks his head a little and a smirk appears on his face.

I hold my breath, not moving a muscle. My lungs are burning from the lack of oxygen.

"Drew, move your ass back to your post and watch for those low life motherfuckers. I want dibs on their Prez. That little shit son of mine will pay for overthrowing me." Chains orders.

Drew turns on his heels and heads back out the door. Chains stands there for a few more seconds and I'm dizzy from holding my breath. He walks away and I gulp in oxygen as fast as I can.

"Shit, we have to warn Blayze," I whisper. I don't want to raise my voice in case they're waiting around the corner. I pat my pockets looking for my phone. "Shit, I left my phone in the car."

"What are we going to do now?" Daisy whispers back.

"Go forward with the plan. Get Danyella and get out." I crouch and slowly move forward. "You can stay here if you want, Daisy. I don't want you to get caught. Go back to the car, lock the doors and stay down."

"Are you sure?" She sounds relieved and scared.

"Yes. If I'm caught, I want you to get out of here. Give me twenty minutes. If I'm not out by then, drive as fast and as far as you can. Don't stop for anyone. Then call Blayze and tell him everything."

"You need to know where to go." I wait for her to find her strength to continue. She closes her eyes. "Go down the stairs and once you reach the bottom, you'll come to a door. Go through that door, walk all the way to the end. You'll come to another door. There will be a dripping of some sort that's hard to hear if there's a lot of footsteps. Turn left after the second door. Count fourteen steps. You'll hear a buzz like noise that reminds you of electricity. Turn right. Open that door. Count another thirty steps." Daisy opens her eyes and stares right at me. "There will be a cage-like door that you have to open. Once you're inside the cage, turn to the left. All the way in the back is where Danyella and I stayed. There are three cots side by side."

"Ok got it." I turn to head down the stairs.

"Monica?"

"Yes?"

"Please, be careful. There's usually a guard or two at each door, I think. They usually blind folded us when they needed to bring us up. So, counting and listening is the only way I knew how to get in and out of there."

"I will. Thank you."

"Oh, and Monica?"

I turn back around. I might be close to losing my patience, but Daisy doesn't deserve that. "What?"

"If there's a little girl with Danyella, can you bring her too? Danyella and I kind of took her under our wing." Tears are forming in Daisy's eyes.

"Yes, I will. I can't bring anyone else though."

"That's fine. The rest of them aren't very nice anyway."

"Go to the car and give me twenty minutes when you get there. Remember what I said. If I'm not out, call Blayze and tell him everything."

Daisy comes to me at a fast pace and hugs me hard. "I will. Be safe."

"You too, Daisy. I'll see you soon." I hug her back. I release her and hurry down the stairs. If I stayed there, she'd keep on procrastinating and I want to get this shit over with and be back in the safety of my home and in the arms of my man.

Once I reach the bottom of the stairs, I follow Daisy's directions. There are no guards at the first door. I slowly open it and slip into the shadows. I look right and then left. Both ways have a long hallway. Then I remember Daisy said to go straight.

I slowly approach the deserted hallway, trying to keep my steps light and silent so I don't alert anyone I'm here. Voices echo down the dirty corridor and I look around to see if there's anywhere I can hide. Not finding anything, I quickly walk to the next door. There is a room to the left with a door wide open and a TV playing a show at a deafening volume.

I peek inside the door and almost lose my stomach. There's a man from Bloody Scorpions sitting in a chair, jacking off while a girl is forced to dance in front of him. I want to stick my knife in his ear and puncture his brain for what he's doing. Grunts and moans fill the room and I step away. If I kill him now, I'll alert everyone else I'm here. I'll finish him on my way out.

I step away from the door and hurry to the heavy metal door Daisy told me about. I'm almost to Danyella. I turn the knob and it gives way under my hands. I pull my knife out of my back just in case it's a trap. When no alarms go off, I turn left and count my steps. Once I reach fourteen, I turn. The buzz like noise is distant but I hear it. In front of me is an open door. I slowly approach it and there's one man with the Bloody Scorpions cut on. His back is to me so I sneak to the left and wait in the shadows. He turns on his heels and walks in my direction. I hold my breath and steady my heartbeat. He walks right past me and out the door, heading the way I just came. Holy shit, that was close.

I count out thirty steps and look left then right. There's a door slightly ajar to my left and I walk that way. Inside is the most heartbreaking thing I've ever seen. So many girls are cuffed to their beds. Their backs are to me, so they have no idea I'm here. It looks like most of them are sleeping. The smell of urine and feces is strong and I have to cover my nose from the stench. Faint cries pierce the quiet room. I hurry to the cage and pick the old lock. Once the tumbles move, freeing the door, I slip inside. I don't lock it, but I do close it just in case that Bloody Scorpions member comes back. No one pays any attention to me. It's like they all lost hope. I head in the direction Daisy told me she stayed with Danyella.

What I see next buckles my knees and I almost fall from a broken heart. Danyella's hand is cuffed to the bed, but she's stretched as far as she can go, curled up on another cot, holding a crying child. Her back is to me, trying to soothe the little girl.

I approach Danyella carefully, not to startle her. "Danyella," I whisper.

Her skinny body stiffens, and she slowly turns her head. The once vibrant green eyes, I'm used to seeing are gone. Instead, they're cold and defeated.

"What do you want?" Danyella snarls. "I'm trying to keep her quiet. Leave me the hell alone."

I approach her and the little girl so she can see me. "It's me, Monica. I'm here to get the two of you out."

"Monica? How'd you? Where'd you?" She exhales a deep breath. "Oh, never mind. I've lost my mind again. There's no way Monica would be here."

"But I am. I'm going to uncuff you and her and we're going to get out of here." I hurry to where her hand is outstretched and pick the cuffs.

Once the spring releases, Danyella snatches her hand and soothes it over the little girls' head. "Shh… it's ok baby girl. I'm not going to let them hurt you."

I uncuff the little girl and reach down to help her up. She's light as a feather in my arms. "Danyella, come on. We have to go before the guard comes back."

Heavy footsteps alert me that it's too late. He's already on his way back. "You have to hide. Please, Monica. If they see you, they'll torture you to get to Capone." Danyella pleads.

I put the little girl on the bed and look around. There's nowhere to go but under the beds. "Is this still Daisy's?"

"Yes. How do you know her?" Danyella asks. There's a panic in her voice.

"That's how I found you. I'll explain later. Act natural and I'll hide under her bed."

Danyella slips her cuff back on but doesn't latch it all the way. She does the same to the little girl and lays back down. I slide under Daisy's cot and wait. The footsteps are getting closer. I close my eyes and send up a prayer to the biker God's that if they can hear me, this guy will move on. The footsteps are right at the cage doors, I can see him from here. He's the first guy in the room with the other girl. I don't have time to think about where she is when he rattles the bars.

"Whoever's still awake, you're going to come join us in a few minutes." He sneers, grabbing his nasty dick in the process. No one moves or makes a sound. He turns and walks away.

I slide out of my hiding spot not thinking about what I was laying in and help Danyella with the little girl. Danyella's too weak to hold onto her. I tuck the little girl's face in my shoulder and turn to Danyella, "Come on, follow me. I might need you to take her if we run into any problems."

Danyella nods. Together we quietly walk to the cage door. I push it open and Danyella takes a hesitant step. She's terrified of what will happen if we're caught. I squeeze her hand, giving her moral support. "It's ok," I whisper. "I got you. I got both of you." Danyella steps all the way out and I close the door and relock it.

We hurry back the way we came, no guards in sight. This is too easy. I keep alert with every step we take. Once we're up the stairs and outside, I take a deep breath, inhaling the clean scent of the city.

I don't stop at the room where the Bloody Scorpion was. It was shut and I didn't want to jeopardize Danyella's life. Once we reach the safety of my car, Daisy is out of the passenger seat and hugging Danyella. The two of them are silently crying and holding onto each other tight.

"Girls, I hate to be the asshole, but we have to move," I say wiping tears from my eyes.

Daisy releases Danyella. She opens the back door and looks at me while Danyella slides in. "Thank you."

Shots ring out and Daisy is thrown against the side of the car. I don't know how bad she's hurt. Danyella screams and the little girl in my arms wails uncontrollably. Danyella grabs Daisy and pulls her in the car. I shove the little girl into the back seat and pull out my gun. My body turns numb as I fire back blindly into the dark alley.

A bullet whizzes by my head and that snaps me back into reality. I have to get these girls out of here safely. I throw myself into the driver's seat and peel out. Tings of bullets against metal pierce the car. I find my phone sitting on the passenger seat and I grab it while trying to keep us on the road. I dial Blayze and he picks up on the first ring.

"Monica. What on earth?"

"Blayze, I need help. Daisy's been shot."

"Where are you?"

"I'm on the corner of 6th and Lambert, heading back to our clubhouse."

"OK, Dagger will be there waiting. You and I will be having a little conversation when I get there." He growls.

"Xander, I have Danyella. But it's bad. I mean really bad. Bloody Scorpions have all those women in a cage, handcuffed to beds. I've never seen anything like it before in my life. We have to help them." My voice trembles.

"What you need to do is get the girls back to the clubhouse now. We'll handle the Bloody Scorpions." Blayze is still so pissed off right now.

"I'm on my way. And in case I haven't told you, I love you, Xander."

"I love you too, Bug. Don't ever pull this shit again." He hangs up the phone before I can say anything else.

"How is she?" I ask, looking in my rearview mirror.

Danyella has tears rolling down her cheeks and she shakes her head. "I'm so sorry, Daisy. I'm so sorry. This shouldn't have happened to you." Danyella sobs. She hugs Daisy's limp body to her chest. The little girl holds Danyella around her neck, soothing her.

Bright lights gain their way behind me. "Shit, hang on," I shout. The lights get brighter and closer until they're right on my bumper. I push the gas harder, trying to outrun them. Traffic ahead of me hits their brakes for a red light and I know if I stop, we're all dead. I gun the gas and cut into the other lane. Horns blare and lights glare at me as I weave in and out of oncoming traffic. I let off the gas at the next intersection, brake hard and crank the wheel hard to the left, drifting around the corner.

Another car comes up to the driver's side of me once I pull out of the drift. This one is a silver Ford Shelby GT 500. The driver is a stunning blonde-haired woman I've seen before. She gives me a wink before falling back and cutting the car off trying to ram me. Another car appears on my right. This one is a dark red Nissan GT-R. The man driving has dark skin and dark hair with blonde highlights. He too offers me a wink and points to a silver Dodge Challenger SRT Hellcat in front of me. He then drops back and stays side by side with the Shelby, blocking the other car chasing me from passing them. I follow the Dodge Challenger into the night, flying down the highway. I don't know these people, but they just saved my life and for that, I'll be forever grateful.

Once we reach the safety of the clubhouse, the gates immediately roll open. The Silver Hellcat I was following enters first. Then me, the silver Shelby and the dark red Nissan. I pull into a parking spot and shut the car off. The others do the same. They climb out of their cars and wait for direction. The driver of the Hellcat is a little Mexican woman with dark hair and deep brown eyes. The man driving the Nissan stays next to her. Danyella is still crying in the back seat, holding onto Daisy and the little girl. The side door Daisy and I came out of a few hours ago flies open and Dagger comes running in our direction followed by the prospect who was hitting on Daisy.

"I'll be right back," I say to Danyella. She nods her head and doesn't say a word. I open the door and meet Dagger and the prospect in the middle of the parking lot. "There's no point." Tears fall rapidly down my face and I don't wipe them away. I hold my head high and grieve for a young lady who lost her life all too soon. God gained an angel today while we lost a beautiful soul.

Dagger ignores me and hurries to the waiting car. The woman driving the Shelby approaches me as I watch Dagger carefully remove Daisy's limp body from the back seat. When she gets close enough, I realize who she is. She's one of the most stunning women I've ever seen. I was immediately envious of her when she came to my studio with The Savage Saints. Her California kissed skin and blonde hair would make anyone jealous. The man standing behind her crosses his arms. He's tall and built like a fighter. He doesn't say much, but he has the same haunted expression in his eyes I've had in mine before.

"Are you OK?" her sweet voice has me in more tears.

"Thank you for saving me." I choke out.

"It was no problem. I live for that shit." She shrugs her shoulders nonchalantly.

"I'm Monica." I offer her my hand. "I owe you a debt for saving my life."

She takes my hand and gives it a firm shake. "I look forward to it. Name's Krimson."

Chapter 9

Blayze

Riding with my brothers is the best feeling in the world. The wind whipping around me. The power of my Harley vibrating with every twist of my wrist. The way I can let go of all the shit happening and focus on the open road. It centers my mind. Centers my soul.

We're riding in formation down the PCH. Some of us will be heading into downtown LA while the rest of us go to the Bloody Scorpions clubhouse. The sun has set fully over the ocean view to my right. Time is ticking down. Capone is in the lead. I'm right behind him to his left and Torch is next to me. Behind me are Bear and Trigger, followed by Tiny, Red and Derange. Two prospects are behind them driving the vans to export the girls to our clubhouse. The traffic isn't as heavy as normal. It's like commuters know something's up and decided to stay home. They'd be right. A war is brewing and we're the bombs ticking down, ready to explode.

Capone lifts his right hand in the air, holding up three fingers. Signaling to our brothers this is where we part. Bear speeds up and gets next to me while Torch slows down to ride with the rest. We turn left and put two fingers facing down as our brothers pass. It's a sign of respect and good luck to keep two wheels on the ground at all times. Once the vans catch up to the three of us,

Capone signals to pull off in an empty parking lot. I check the time we have left until the auction. There's a little over two hours to go.

Capone pulls into a parking spot at the way back of the lot and turns his bike off. Bear and I follow. The prospects driving the vans cage us in and block us from the view of the road. Capone climbs off his bike, removes his brain bucket and lights up a smoke. The ticking of our cooling bikes is the only noise in the quiet night.

"Prez, what's going on?" I ask as I climb off my bike and remove my brain bucket. I really want to get to the old warehouse to scope it out before it's too late. My nerves are on the edge of exploding and taking my frustration out on my Prez and best friend.

"I got a text before we left. The instructions said to meet here." Capone responds.

"Text? From who? What the hell, Prez?" I growl. I suck in a breath when the words leave my lips. Fuck I just screwed up.

Capone levels me with a glare and inhales his cigarette. He blows the smoke out before addressing my disrespect. "First, I'm going to let that fucking slide because I know how stressed you are. Second, my decisions are not to be questioned. Krimson asked me to stay here until we get the all clear to move forward. Remember your place Blayze. My fucking Club. My decisions. End of fucking discussion. Are we clear VP?" Capone drops his cigarette and grinds it out with his boot.

"Aye, Prez. Sorry about that. It won't happen again." Shit, I'm lucky on that one. I have to learn how to pick my battles with him and this wasn't one of them.

My phone buzzes in my pocket and I yank it out of my jeans. Capone's does the same. It's the gate alarm at the clubhouse. Someone either just arrived or left. I pull up the camera and what I see makes my blood boil. My girl is hurrying back to the black Dodge Charger and exiting the clubhouse.

"What the hell is she doing?" I ask no one in particular. I knew we should've hidden all the car keys. I look up to Capone and he's watching the same video. The slight tick in his jaw is the only sign he's pissed.

I close out of the security app and dial her number. It rings a few times before sending me to voicemail. "Bug. Answer your damn phone." I growl when it beeps to leave a message. My fingers tighten on my phone causing it to crack under the pressure.

Capone dials her number and the same thing happens. "Monica, get back into the clubhouse. Now." He hangs up and I dial again.

"Voicemail, again." Motherfucker.

We both try a few more times until it now goes directly to voicemail. What in the hell is she doing? I will blister that ass so hard; she'll be able to feel me for a week when she sits down.

"What do we do now Prez?" Rage settles deep into my bones. I need my President to guide me before I go off the rails.

"We continue with the plans and wait for my contact to show up and give us the all clear." Capone levels me with a stare so cold, I shiver. "I don't know what my sister is up to, but she's a big girl and can handle herself. I need you to focus on what we're doing, not worry about what she's doing. Can you do that, Blayze? Because if you can't, hop on your bike and head back to the clubhouse. We're going to war and need all your attention before one of us gets killed."

I close my eyes and inhale a deep breath, centering my mind. Capone is right. I can't control Monica no matter how much I want to. She can handle whatever she's doing and if she can't, she'll call. I have to trust that. Trust her. Opening my eyes, I nod at my Prez, "Aye. I'm here and ready to take these fuckers down. You have my word." I reply. "Good. I know this isn't your strong suit, but now we wait." He turns to Bear still sitting on his bike. I forgot he was even here. "You good with that Bear?" Capone asks. "Aye, Prez. I'm ready to move forward on your word." Bear responds.

We sit in silence and wait. Capone paces back and forth in front of his bike, checking his phone every few steps. Bear remains on his bike, not saying much or moving. He's focused on the mission. I keep checking my cracked phone every few minutes, hoping Bug is safe. The heat from the day radiating off the pavement, wrapping itself around me. That's one thing I love about California. The heat. Some days it can be down right sweltering outside where your skin will fall off from sweating and a few days later you need jeans and a hoodie. Capone's right, this isn't my strong suit. Waiting sucks. All I want to do is go in there and slice every motherfucker around from groin to throat and watch their insides tumble out. That's the reason I earned the road name Blayze. I head into danger with my guns blazing. I shoot first and ask questions later.

I've always been a stubborn ass and will continue that way until the day I die. It's ingrained in my DNA. My father was a member of the old Royal Bastards MC when Chains was the Prez. He was killed during the war. A casualty that sucked but it's the way this life goes. Once you choose your side, you choose what happens next. And his betrayal to Capone ended his life. I have no idea where my mother is. She high tailed it out of this life when me and my sister were preteens. Leaving us with the club bunnies and Ol' Ladies to look after us. My dad tried his best raising us. Danyella and I are only ten months apart and what some people call Irish twins. I wasn't even a month old when my father knocked my mother up for the second time. One thing I remember from him is that he liked to fuck. He enjoyed getting his dick wet any way he could. He was one of the most unfaithful bastards around. I think that's one reason why my mother left. She just one day up and disappeared without a word or a trace of where she went.

"Any idea how much longer?" I ask.

Capone looks at his phone for the hundredth time. "Should be soon. It's getting closer to midnight. Krimson said she'd have us in there before the auction starts."

My phone vibrates in my hand. Monica's name appears on the screen. I quickly swipe accept and put the phone up to my ear. "Monica, what on earth?"

"Blayze, I need help. Daisy's been shot." Monica's voice trembles with every word. I can hear her driving fast.

"Where are you?" I signal to Capone and put the phone on speaker.

"I'm on the corner of 6th and Lambert and heading back to the clubhouse." Monica is on the verge of a breakdown and I need to keep her calm.

"OK, Dagger will be there waiting. You and I will be having a little conversation when I get there." I growl.

"Xander, I have Danyella. But it's bad. I mean really bad. Bloody Scorpions have all those women in a cage, handcuffed to beds. I've never seen anything like it before in my life. We have to help them." Her voice is a quivering mess.

I do my best to keep her sane. "What you need to do is get the girls back to the clubhouse now. We'll handle the Bloody Scorpions." I'm so pissed off right now. She put herself in danger and now that little girl is hurt.

"I'm on my way. And in case I haven't told you, I love you, Xander." She sighs into the phone.

"I love you too, Bug. Don't ever pull this shit again." I hang up the phone before she can say anything else.

I throw my brain bucket on and look at Capone. He's on the phone pacing back and forth nodding every few seconds. I'm sure he doesn't realize he's doing that. Whoever he's talking to can't see him nod. Capone hangs up the phone after a few beats and hurries over to his bike. He throws his helmet on and starts his bike.

"We're going in hard, boys. Take out anyone standing in our way. Krimson and her crew will get the girls back to the clubhouse safely. We need to focus on what we're doing." He shouts over the rumble of his bike. I confirm with a nod and fire up my bike. Bear does the same. Capone peels out of the parking lot. Bear and I are right behind him, shifting gears hard. The vans with the prospects are right behind us, not giving anyone room on either side of the two-lane roads. The five of us fly through the streets of L.A. not stopping for red lights or slowing down for anything.

We make it to the old warehouse and Capone pulls down an alley next to a backdoor that's left wide open. I shut my bike off, dismount and pull my .40 caliber out of my cut, ready to blow any motherfucker up that gets in my way. I quickly remove my helmet. Capone and Bear are doing the same. The two prospects driving the vans approach us.

Capone turns his attention to them, "Prospects, we need you both with us. Once we start letting the girls out, then you take off and head right for the clubhouse. Don't stop for anything or anyone."

"Got it." They say in unison.

"Be ready to shed some blood boys. If you can't do that then pack your shit and get the fuck out of my Club." Capone is ready to take these fuckers down. "This separates the men from the boys. There's no turning back once we enter. You all ready?" Capone looks to each of us, waiting to see who's going to back out.

I already have my gun drawn and a knife in my other hand. I'm ready. Bear has his gun ready and a whip in his other hand. The two prospects have their guns out and each has their own knife. I give Capone a nod.

"Take each fucker out silently unless it's absolutely necessary to use your gun. I don't care if you break their necks, slice them open or however you need to. Do it quietly."

"Aye, Prez. We're ready. Let's get these motherfuckers." I answer. Bear and the two prospects nod in agreement. My adrenaline is pumping through my veins. I live for this shit.

Capone is the first one through the metal door. I follow close behind, searching for a sign someone is in the stairwell. Capone points to the stairs and we head down to the basement at a rapid pace. We go to the first door and it's locked. Capone steps off to the side and I pick the lock. Once the tumblers release, I slowly open the door and my gun aimed out. It's silent down the long corridor.

"What the fuck?" I whisper to Capone. My voice echoes down the dirty hallway. He shushes me with his hand and walks straight down the hallway, keeping to the walls. I see a light at the end and hear people talking. Once we reach it, it's another metal door. There's a small hallway to the right and another door that's slightly ajar to where the voices are coming from.

Capone points me to the open door and I sneak down that way. I press my back against the wall and push the door open a little wider. The television is at a loud volume playing some sitcoms. I don't pay attention to what's on. I'm looking at a Bloody Scorpions member sitting in a chair, his back to me, groping a girl dancing for him. Her moves are choppy and her body is trembling. She's wearing a dirty tank top, short shorts and nothing else on her malnourished frame. He grabs her hips and yanks her down onto his lap.

"That's enough teasing you little slut. Now suck me off." He sends her to her knees on the dirty carpet. She has tears in her eyes when he unbuckles his pants and pulls himself out stroking it. "Real deep and dirty, slut. You know how I like it."

Before the girl can even blink, I'm behind him. I hold my knife to his throat and yank his head back so he can see who's ending his life.

"You can't do this," the Bloody Scorpion grunts. His hand is still on his dick.

"I wish I could take the time to play with you like you were playing with her, but I won't. Tell me where the rest of them are." My voice is low and deadly when I glare into his eyes and press my knife into his throat. Just enough to break the skin.

"Fuck you. You're all dead." He spits out.

"No, you're dead." I sink my knife into his throat and cover his mouth with my free hand so he can't scream and alert the others. I watch as his blood spills down his shirt and the life drains from his eyes. Once he stops moving, staring up lifelessly, I remove my hand. I wipe his blood off my knife on his jeans and drag his body to the corner. The girl is still kneeling on the carpet, watching everything I'm doing. She hasn't said a word.

I approach her slowly, my hands out in front of me to show I'm not a threat, "Are you OK?" She nods her head but doesn't move. "Do you know where the others are? We're here to help."

She nods her head and rises. "I can show you if you promise to get us out of here. There are four of those men here tonight." The girls voice is quiet and timid.

"Yes, we're going to get you all out. How many girls?" I lead the way back to where Capone, Bear and the two Prospects are.

"There's at least twenty of us down here. There used to be more, but some have disappeared and never returned." Sadness laces her voice.

Capone steps forward, "We're going to get you all out. Can you show us where everyone is?"

"Yes. Follow me." She takes off to the left and we hurry to keep up with her. She walks a few more paces and turns right. There's an open door in front of us. "Through that door is the cage. There's one guard." She points to the open door.

"Stay behind me. We'll go first, then I'll need your help to get them to trust us." Capone orders. The girl stays against the wall and waits.

Capone peers inside and then disappears. A grunt followed by a heavy body hitting the floor comes out of that room. I peer inside and see Capone moving a Bloody

Scorpion to the side. A blood trail following him. He grabs a set of keys off the key ring attached to his belt.

"Come on. It's clear." Capone orders.

I enter the room first and the smell hits me like a freight train before I reach the cage. Shit and piss linger in the air. Once I reach the cage, my stomach revolts from the sight before me. Rows upon rows of cots are lined up against the walls. Women are handcuffed to each bed. Some are sitting up looking at us in fright. Others are laying down with their backs to us like they've given up on all hope.

"Capone, bring that girl in," I shout. That gets some of the girls moving on the cots. Sobs and sniffles penetrate the quiet room.

"Holy fuck. This is sick." Capone says when he steps up next to me. He covers his mouth to try and stop the smell. "Let's get these girls out."

Capone uses the key and unlocks the cage doors. The girl I rescued hurries past us and heads straight to a cot near the back to the left occupied by another girl. She gently shakes her awake. "Kensi, these guys are here to help us. Wake up."

The girl named Kensi opens her eyes and turns toward us. Her eyes widen when she sees us. "I knew you'd come." A smile plays on her face. "Dany told us you'd find her. It's really happening. We're getting out of here." She tugs on her cuff trying to get free.

Capone hurries over to the girl and unlocks her handcuff. "You know Danyella?"

She nods her head and looks to the empty cot next to her. Tears fall down her face "Where is she?"

"She's safe. We're going to get you all out of here." Capone reassures her.

"Wait. How many guards did you get rid of?"

"Two. Why?"

"There are two more, a man wearing a thick chain around his neck and a skinny guy they call J.J. You have to get rid of them or they'll call the others and kill us all." Her bottom lip trembles.

Capone glances at me and I leave the room with a prospect on my heels. Together the two of us head back in the direction we came from. Once we reach the stairs, I hear heavy footsteps above us and a voice I'll never forget.

"Get the girls and move them to the next location. We've been breached by my bitch of a daughter." Chains growls. Footsteps approach us at a rapid pace. I can't count how many because of the echo they produce.

The prospect and I hunker down, waiting for them to approach. Once three men come into view, I spring up from my crouched position and gut the first one wearing a Bloody Scorpion cut. My knife sinks into his stomach and I pull up, the jagged edge of my blade ripping his skin apart. The prospect has another Scorpion down. He pulls his knife out of the guy's throat. The third man tries to run back up the stairs but I'm on him before he makes it two steps. My fist lands hard to the back of his head, stunning him. He sways before he regains his bearings and attempts to get away again. I grab his cut and slam his head into the concrete wall repeatedly. Blood gushes from his face meeting the concrete. I hold onto him and the prospect approaches us and slices his throat, ending his life.

"Three down, two to go. Good work prospect." I praise as I drop the Blood Scorpions body to the ground.

I shove him out of the way and text Capone.

Me: Stairwell clear. Heading up to eliminate two more.

Capone: Copy that. We're right behind you.

We make our way up the stairs quietly. Once we reach the landing where we came in, I turn to the left. The door is ajar, and I silently point to it. The prospect nods his head and together we enter, staying in the shadows. I see Chains pacing back and forth in the middle of the floor. He has a limp and he looks old. Ridden hard and put away wet. I thought Capone ended him after he attacked Monica.

"Something's wrong. I don't know what yet, but I can feel it." Chains barks.

John James, Monica's ex, comes out of the shadows. He has bruising under his eyes and his nose is crooked from where she broke it. "You're paranoid old man. Nothing's wrong."

Chains levels him with a glare. "I trust my gut. It's how I survived when Capone thought he killed me." Chains continues to pace back and forth with his limp. His movements are slow and it appears he's in pain.

I pull out my phone and text Capone again.

Me: Need you up here quick. Stay quiet. You're not going to believe what I'm seeing.

Capone: On my way.

Me: In the room to the left of the top stairwell where we came in.

Capone: Copy that.

The prospect and I hunker down and wait for Capone to get up here. I keep my eyes on John and Chains. They're in a heated debate about something, but I can't hear what they're saying because they're whispering. They keep looking at the door we came in through. John moves closer to where I'm hiding in the shadows.

Capone slips inside. His eyes grow wide when he sees Chains standing in the middle of the floor, not moving from his spot at the door. Chains glances over and spots Capone standing there.

"You're dead, old man," Capone growls. He pulls his gun up and aims it at Chains' head.

"No, you thought I was dead. As you can see, I'm very much alive and I'm going to kill you." Chains responds, pulling his gun and aiming it at my President. John tries to sneak out, but he heads in my direction. No time for hesitation now. I come out of the shadows and head right for John. His eyes widen in fright. I'm across the floor in a few quick strides and grab him by the front of his shirt, lifting his scrawny frame off the floor. I slam him into the wall behind him when I hear a gunshot ring out. I turn my head with my hand wrapped around John's throat. Chains falls to the ground, a bullet in his brain.

"He's dead now." Capone's voice is mellow with no remorse. The only time I've heard him talk this way is when he's lost in the chaos of taking a life. The only way he'll come back is to work the aggression off in the ring.

The weasel dick motherfucker I have pinned to the wall is trying to claw at me to release my grip, turning my attention back to him.

"What are you going to do with me?" John asks. His voice is high and ragged. I relax my grip just a little so he can breathe.

"We're going to have some fun with you." I slam his head against the wall and he falls unconscious after one hit. "Pussy." I drop John's body to the floor and secure his hands and feet with zip ties. I gag him and cover his eyes with a bandanna.

"Prospect, put him in the van and make sure he's away from the girls. We don't want them scared any more than what they are." I order. "And if he wakes up, knock his ass out again."

"You got it VP." The prospect drags John's unconscious body out the door. He isn't gentle with him.

I approach Capone and rest a hand on his shoulder. "Brother, you good?" I know he isn't right now, but I hope I can break through the chaos his head is in.

"I will be." Capone shrugs off my hand and approaches Chains' lifeless body. He kneels down next to him and searches his pockets. He pulls out a cell phone, his wallet and a photo.

"What are you looking for?"

"I'm not sure, but if Chains was alive, that means he might have been behind the shit with Los Demons." He unfolds the picture.

I look at it and my stomach sinks to my toes. Rage vibrates through my body. "Holy fuck."

"Yeah, brother. Holy fuck."

Chapter 10

Blayze

Once we get all the girls loaded into the vans, Capone and I ride straight to the Bloody Scorpions clubhouse. Bear left with the vans to make sure they get to our place safely. The picture Chains had on him still makes my blood boil.

Capone has been too quiet during the whole thing and I know what he's thinking. He's thinking the same thing as I am. Someone has some serious explaining to do.

We arrive at the meeting spot about a half a mile away from Bloody Scorpions clubhouse and shut off our bikes. The wind picks up leaving a chill down my spine. This will be another blood bath. We dismount and find our guys. Derange, Trigger, Torch, Red and Tiny are waiting in the woods surrounding the clubhouse. They have a perfect angle for watching the Bloody Scorpions and they don't even know we're here. My brothers are looking at Capone, waiting for direction from our Prez, but I know he isn't in the right frame of mind to lead anyone right now. He wants bloodshed and wants it now.

Capone doesn't say a word. He's staring at the clubhouse ready to seek revenge, so I take the lead. "Give us the details."

"Two guys outside, rotating every hour on the hour. The rest are inside and from the sounds of it, they're having a party." Red answers.

"Eliminate the two outside quietly. We need a distraction to draw the rest of the guys out. Get them away from the innocents inside."

Torch smiles, "I have an idea." That crazy look he has isn't good for them. I've seen it before and we had the Fire Marshall up our ass for a few weeks. Fuck it.

"Go do your thing, Torch." I give him the go ahead. He disappears into the night, whistling a tune. I shake my head, turning my attention back to the guards outside. They're strapped with AK47's pacing back and forth along the porch. One walks to the left and the other to the right. Once they reach the edge of the open porch, they turn back. "How long do we have before they rotate."

"Twenty minutes." Red answers.

The guys are looking at Capone, concern in their eyes. I need to snap him out of this rage brewing before we go in. Our brothers need their leader. I grab Capone by the shoulders and pull him away from the rest of the guys.

"Capone, pull yourself together." I step into his space, trying to get a reaction out of him.

"Fuck you, Blayze." Capone's jaw ticks with every beat.

"Look, I get it. I do. But we can't fix that now and your men need you. They need you to direct and lead them. Don't puss out on them now."

"Fuck off. I'm not." He clenches and unclenches his fists. The rage burning in his eyes would make a sane man back off. No one said I was sane. It's why I'm the V.P. My job is to keep my Prez's head in the game.

"You are. You're being a little bitch right now." I get in Capone's face. "Not the President we all know you are. You're letting your emotions run you. They can see it. So, get it the fuck together. Then once this is settled you can crack some skulls."

Capone closes his eyes for a brief second before opening them again. The glint in his eyes returns. "You're right. Let's kill these fuckers then deal with that."

I slap him on the back. "Exactly, Prez. These are your men and they need you now."

"Thanks, Blayze."

"That's what I'm here for." I shrug my shoulders.

Turning back, we reach the guys and Capone takes the lead. "We're going in and going hard. No mercy on any of these dick bags. If you witnessed what we'd seen, you'd understand. They had at least twenty women and little girls chained to beds forced to sit in their own piss and shit. They were all undernourished, raped and beaten. Danyella talked about us and she never gave up hope and she spread that through the rest of the girls. They never gave up hope." Capone takes a second to gather his emotions. "They're currently heading to our clubhouse, safe. We killed four of their men, captured one and killed someone who I thought was already dead."

"Who?" Trigger asks.

Capone blinks a few times before answering. "We captured John James and I ended Chains' life for the second time."

"I thought he was already dead after what he did to Monica?" Red questions.

"I thought so too. It appears Chains had connections to another MC that we didn't know about.

This MC." Capone points to the Bloody Scorpions clubhouse. "They must have snatched him up when I left him for dead. But no matter how much protection he had; he's now dancing with the devil with a bullet in his brain."

A movement toward their clubhouse catches our attention. Torch is moving silently between each bike parked off to the side next to an old barn. I'm not sure what he's up to, but I know it's going to be huge. "Come on, let's move and end these motherfuckers," I say pulling out my gun and knife.

Trigger, Red, Derange, Tiny and Capone all get ready for battle. Capone leads us to the back of their clubhouse, sticking to the shadows. Trigger, Tiny and Red head off to the left. Capone, Derange and I head to the opposite side. One guard walks our way. Once he reaches the end of the porch, I leave my spot against the house, come up behind him and sink my blade into his throat, dragging his flaying body to the side of the clubhouse.

"Welcome to hell, motherfucker." The guard gurgles with blood trailing past his lips and onto his cut. He takes his last breath and slumps to the ground.

"Clear," I whisper to Capone and whistle to let the other guys know.

I wait for a beat and the whistle is returned. Trigger, Tiny and Red eliminated the other guard. We all meet in front of the clubhouse, staying low. Hiding behind a couple of trucks, we wait for Torch to do his work. He comes running toward us with a grin on his face. Once he reaches us an explosion rings out. All the Blood Scorpions' bikes are up in flames. If that doesn't draw these assholes out, nothing will.

As the fire burns, we wait. A few minutes later, the clubhouse door flies open and their men come running out yelling and screaming. Some are half-naked carrying fire extinguishers, others are naked. None of them are armed.

"It's show time. Let's show these assholes why you don't fuck with the Royal Bastards." Capone shouts.

I fire into the crowd, hitting a few. One tries to sneak back in and I put a bullet in his brain. We open fire on the unsuspecting MC killing everyone in sight. Bodies are falling in rapid succession. One after another, after another. Each member of the Bloody Scorpions are laying in a heap on the ground. Their blood soaking the earth. They've been eliminated but a gut feeling is telling me this was too easy. The weirdest part is that there was no screaming from inside from the rest of the partiers. There should've been some innocents.

"We did it. They're done." Tiny shouts.

"Let's get out of here before the fire department shows up." Torch suggests.

"Wait." Capone raises a hand stopping their celebration. "Something isn't right. We need to check out the clubhouse. Clear it before we go."

"Lead the way, Prez." I agree.

Capone heads to the front of the house and steps over a body. I follow close behind and take in the wreckage we left behind. Bodies are scattered everywhere, smoke from the bikes lingering in the air. Capone reaches the front door and kicks the flimsy wood. It gives way on the first try and flies open, banging against the side of the house. He goes in first, gun drawn. I follow.

Looking around the Bloody Scorpions clubhouse, bile rises in my throat. The first thing that hits me is the smell. It smells just like the basement that the girls were kept in. These nasty fuckers obviously don't know how to clean. In front of me is the common room with old furniture scattered all around. Metal cages big enough for a girl to be in are suspended from the ceiling, empty.

To my left is the bar and kitchen. Red and Tiny head that way, clearing those rooms in the back. There's a set of stairs to my right that go up to the rooms. Torch and Derange head that way. Trigger sticks with Capone and me as we carefully walk past the common room and the swinging cages. I cover my mouth with my gloved hand, trying to stop the smell from making me nauseous.

Capone enters a room in the back and points to a door. I grab the handle and twist, pushing it open. It's another basement and the smell is worse this way.

"What the fuck is wrong with these people?" I flip on a light switch and the stairs light up with dim bulbs. I lead the way down the rickety old staircase. Each step creaks under my weight. Once I reach the bottom, I turn left. "You've got to be fucking kidding me."

Capone steps up next to me, looking around. "Thank fuck each of those sick assholes are dead."

"What do we do now?" Trigger asks.

"Burn the bitch down. There's nothing we can do for them." Capone turns and heads back up the stairs. "Check the bodies. Just to make sure." He disappears up the stairs leaving Trigger and me.

"This is some sick shit." Trigger says.

We walk deeper into the basement. Against the outside wall are dead girls chained to it. There is a metal chair sitting in the middle of the concrete floor over a drain. Fresh blood coats the concrete. I put my finger against the first girl's neck to check for a pulse. She's cold to the touch. I move onto the next and Trigger does the same. Silently, we check each girl. The hope of finding one alive is waning with each dead body I come across. There are at least ten girls down here chained to the wall, dead. When I reach the last girl toward the back of the basement, my stomach decides to revolt. I put my hands on my legs and lean over, throwing up everything in my stomach. This girl couldn't have been older than fifteen. Her body's still warm to the touch, but she has no pulse. Her lifeless eyes stare right at me. I lose it.

"Son of a bitch," I growl and punch the wall. Tears are welling in my eyes and I wipe them away, breathing erratically. Rage is burning through my body at the sight of all these innocent girls, dead. I want to bring all these motherfuckers back from the dead and kill them all over again.

Trigger approaches me, "I know, brother. But the best thing we can do now is let them rest in peace. Help me unhook them." Together we unchain each girl and lay their lifeless bodies side by side. I close each girls' eyes and say a prayer that their souls rest in peace. Once we're done, Trigger and I stand side by side. I wipe the tears from my eyes and say a final prayer.

"Let your spirit carry on into the afterlife. Let your loved ones know you aren't suffering anymore. An evil brought you down here, but light set you free. Rest in peace, angels. And watch over each other. Amen."

"Amen." Trigger echoes.

We walk up the basement stairs with a slump in our shoulders, defeated. I turn off the light and close the door. Capone is pacing back and forth in the living room. He looks up when we enter.

"Done?"

"Aye, Prez. Done." I respond walking out of the clubhouse. The fresh air hits me in the face and I breathe for the first time since entering that place. I sit down on the steps and wait for them to finish inside. All I want to do is head home to Monica. Let her soothe the anguish resting on my shoulders. Let her heal the carnage and heartache on my soul. I pull out my phone and send her a text.

Blayze: IDK if UR up but I'll be home soon. I need you.

The little bubbles appear and disappear a couple of times before a response comes through.

Bug: I'll be here. I need you too.

Capone comes out of the house and sits down next to me, lighting up a cigarette. He offers me one and I accept. "Torch will be done soon. Once he finishes, this place never existed."

"What are we going to do about the other thing?" I ask.

"We'll deal with that tomorrow. Right now, all I want to do is go home and forget, even if it's for just a little while." Capone's way of forgetting is to be occupied by one of the club bunnies.

"Aye, me too Prez. I want to forget this night ever happened." I inhale my cigarette and exhale the smoke through my nose. "What about these bodies?" I point to the men scattered across the yard.

"Cleaning crew will be here in about ten minutes. Once they dispose of the Bloody Scorpions, they have instructions on how to light this place up. Torch is one crafty motherfucker."

Torch, Trigger, Red and Tiny exit the clubhouse and shut the door. Torch disappears around the back for a couple of minutes and returns.

"Ready, Prez."

"Let's roll. Head back to the clubhouse." Silently we walk back to our bikes. Everyone lost in their own thoughts. Even though we brought down a huge trafficking ring, something still feels off. Something isn't right. And until we get to the bottom of what Chains had on him, this will never end.

Chapter 11

Monica

It's been an hour since I've come back to the clubhouse and cried myself to exhaustion. The tears finally quit falling but there's a sharp pain in my chest. I rub my hand over my heart trying to ease the torture of each beat. I can't believe I did this. This is all on me. I should've left Daisy here. I should've never let her come with me. If I did, then she wouldn't be where she is now. It's all my fault. Every drop of Daisy's blood is on my hands. I slam my fists on the bar where I'm sitting and release a quiet scream. Everything is my fault.

"God damn it." More tears trail down my cheeks. I don't think they'll ever stop.

The only ones here at the clubhouse are a few prospects, some club bunnies, Dagger, Danyella and the little girl who was with her and Daisy. Krimson and her crew stuck around waiting for Capone and Blayze to return. A man named Rush, a Latino woman named Hotflash, Redline, Quickshift and Noah. Then Krimson's boyfriend Nolan and his team. Ashton Iverson, Duane Harris, Keanu Marks and Anthony Ramirez. His team is made up of retired military men who've served their time and got out. They're scattered about the common room, drinking or staring off into space. Danyella took the little girl to her room we kept for her when we got here and I haven't seen them since. Dagger and a prospect have been with Daisy trying to keep her alive. A silence descends upon us. It's like they know the pain on my heart and the torture in my soul. No one's talked to me since we first arrived and I don't blame them. I've lashed out and snapped at anyone who's tried.

I slam my hands on the bar top and stand up. I can't sit here any longer. I have to do something. I have to release this pent-up rage brewing under my skin. Krimson watches me with concern in her honey-colored eyes and I'm sick of the pitying looks. I know it's my fault Daisy is where she is. I know.

"What?" I snap. I don't give a shit if she's some badass chick with a hot as hell guy with her. I don't care if she's taken down the biggest asshole in the racing circuit. This is my home, my club. I'll do and say whatever I want.

"Do you want to talk about it?" Krimson asks. She's being nice and I'm being a raging bitch.

I exhale a deep breath, composing myself. "No, I don't. I already know it's my fault."

"Did you shoot her?" Krimson looks at me patiently.

I stare at her and blink a couple of times. "What?"

"Are you responsible for firing the gun that shot her?"

"No." I cross my arms over my chest. "But I'm responsible for putting her in danger." I'm getting pissed.

"That's not what I asked. Did. You. Shoot. Her?" The punctuation of each word is grating on my nerves.

"No, I didn't shoot her," I growl, shaking my head.

"Then you're not responsible." Krimson rests her hands on my shoulders. "Look, I know you don't know me very well and I don't know you. But trust me when I say this isn't your fault. You're not the one who pulled the trigger. You're not the one who shot her."

"But I brought her with me. If I left her here..." I trail off composing myself so I don't cry again.

Krimson interrupts me before I can finish. "If you left her here, you wouldn't have known where to go. Danyella and that little girl would still be locked away in that basement or sold already. You didn't make her go. She wanted to go and help. This isn't your fault. Once you get past the blame game, you'll see that." Krimson's soft voice rings in my head. She thinks this isn't my fault. But she doesn't understand. It is my fault. "No, Monica. It's not your fault." She looks at Nolan and he gives her a slight nod. "Walk with me?"

"Fine," I motion toward the back of the clubhouse. We walk together out the back door. It's safe back here. None of the club members are around and no one can get past our security to get in. We walk the length of the driveway lit up with floodlights. Once we reach the end, we turn and walk back. The nighttime sounds of crickets and owls can be heard over our footsteps. The warm wind whips around us, cocooning me with its heat.

Krimson wrings her hands together. "When I was a teenager, my family was taken from me in a tragic accident. For years I blamed myself. We were at a race in Palisades Del Ray. My father was on the dirt track winning the race. Rush and I were at the back of the crowd in a heated argument over who hurt him earlier that week when an explosion rang out." Krimson stares off into space like she's remembering that night. "When I realized what happened, I tried to get to the scene. Rush was holding me back. I broke free and what I saw next changed my life. My father's car was burning with him inside. The debris from the explosion landed in the crowd killing my mother and little brother. For years I blamed myself for living when they died." She inhales through her nose and closes her eyes. "I still smell the racing fuel and blood that hung heavily in the air."

"That's terrible, but how is it your fault? You didn't cause the accident." Realization dawns on me. "You're a sneaky bitch."

Krimson opens her eyes and smiles. "And once I stopped blaming myself, I discovered that it wasn't an accident. My dad's business partner wanted him dead so he could take over his territory. Only thing is, he didn't expect me to come back and when I did, I ended his life." The look in her eyes would make anyone tremble with fear. Now I see why they call her Krimson. "Then, I discovered my brother who I thought was dead, well, he wasn't. They took him and kept him from me all those years. He's still alive."

"Where is he now? Does he blame you? Do you talk to him?" I rapid fire questions not giving her a chance to answer.

"At first, he blamed me for leaving him with them. But now? Now we're in a good place. His anger is directed at the dead man who tore our family apart. We talk every day. He's currently going through his own shit, trying to deal with being back in our circuit. But that's his story to tell. He was such a vibrant little boy when they took him away from me. He had the world by the balls." Krimson stops talking and silence descends upon us. It's awkward but manageable. I want to ask more, but the buzz of the security gate breaks the silence. Krimson and I hurry to the edge of the clubhouse to see who's coming in.

The two white vans the guys left with are rolling in and park next to the clubhouse entrance. Bear follows them in on his bike. He parks next to the vans and hurries around to open the back doors. Several women climb out of the vans, looking around scared out of their minds.

Krimson and I hurry over. Our footsteps are loudly slapping on the pavement drawing attention our way. Bear unholsters his weapon and aims in our direction until we come into view. He lowers his weapon and puts it away.

"Monica, we need help with these girls. They're terrified."

"What do you want me to do?" I'm helpless when it comes to keeping people calm. It's not my thing. Once I reach the vans, I see around twenty women and children huddled together, crying. I'm so out of my element. "Let me go get Danyella. Maybe she can help."

One woman steps forward with a spark of hope in her eyes. "You know where Dany is?"

"She's inside in her room. This is her home." I spread my arms wide like I can embrace the clubhouse.

"Do you hear that? Danyella was right." The woman turns to the others huddled around. "Those men were right. We're safe here."

"How can that be? They told us if we ever escaped, they'd kill us and our families. We're all going to die." A teenager with dirty brown hair sobs.

"You're safe here. If you would've just believed me in the first place, you wouldn't doubt what's right in front of you now." Danyella steps out of the building facing these irate women head on. She's showered and changed. Looking more like her old self minus the skin and bones from being underfed.

"Danyella?" The woman who tried to reason with the others steps forward. "It's true? We're safe?"

"Yes, Kensi. We're safe here. I'm going to get you ladies cleaned up, changed and fed. Aerial and I have already done that." The little girl steps forward, she too has showered and changed. The clothes she has on are several sizes too big for her, but she seems happy and comfortable.

"Aeri? Oh my god. Ladies come on. I don't know about you, but I need to wash this filth off." Kensi smiles, lighting up the whole crowd. The other women are hesitant but follow Danyella, Aerial and Kensi inside. I bring up the rear with Krimson next to me. Bear and the two prospects stay with the van. It appears they're debating about something but it's not my concern. Not when there's a clubhouse full of scared women. If they need me, they'll come find me.

We walk down the long corridor into the common room. Four of Nolan's men stop playing pool. Krimson's crew stands up from the couches. Everyone who was doing something stops and watches us enter. The women stay together with their heads down, not making eye contact with anyone. Once they're all at the center of the room, Danyella speaks.

"Ok. Here's what we're going to do. There are three bathrooms to use in this area. You can go two at a time if you want and a prospect will guard the doors so you feel safer. The bathrooms are down that hallway." She points to the left toward our rooms. "Monica and I will get you clean clothes. The other prospects will start cooking for you and when you're done, you come back out here and eat." Danyella looks at me to make sure it's OK. I nod my head. These women would've never listened to me. "Break off into pairs and the first three pairs follow us."

I step up next to Danyella and offer a smile. It's brittle, but the best I can do right now. "Prospects, start cooking," I order. They'll listen to me before Danyella.

"What do you want us to cook?" One asks.

"I really don't give a shit. Make what you'd want to eat after being starved for months, possibly years. Make enough for everyone to have more than one plate." I roll my eyes and snap my fingers. Three of the six set off toward the kitchen. "You three, with us. And if any of you want to try something inappropriate, I'll cut off your balls and shove them down your throat. Then I'll cut off your tiny dicks and send them to your mamas. We clear?"

"Crystal." The three answer in unison. I don't have to worry about it, but I want these women and girls to feel safe here.

Kensi and five girls follow us down the short hallway. We stop at the first bathroom and Danyella opens the door for them. Two enter and close it behind them. I hear the lock click into place. One prospect stands guard outside the door, crossing his arms over his chest. He won't let anything happen to those girls. Danyella comes to the second bathroom door and opens it.

"How big is this place?" Kensi asks.

"Pretty big. Large enough for each of our club members to have a room. Some rooms are designed for families of four or single rooms. That way, the families can be comfortable when we have a lockdown or they want to come stay. Then we have rooms for the club bunnies. Outside we have another building built for boxing and working out. I'd say around sixteen thousand square feet. This whole place used to be a warehouse for storing cars. The Royal Bastards MC bought it around ten years ago, converted it into their clubhouse and we've been here ever since." I answer with pride in my voice. "We also have another area designed as a playroom for the little ones. There are different things to do in there like kids can draw, play and run around like maniacs."

Kensi's eyes grow wide. "Club bunnies?"

"Yeah, the women who want to fu.." I trail off looking at the little girl Aerial, that came with Danyella. Her eyes are wide and she's listening to every word I speak. I quickly change the direction of my next words. "Two consenting adults who want to associate behind closed doors." I look at Danyella and she is covering her mouth, trying to hold back her laughter. Bitch.

"They screw behind closed doors." Aerial proudly states. Gasps fill the hallway and Danyella covers Aerial's mouth with her hand before she can say anything else. Aerial removes Danyella's hand and shrugs her shoulders. "It's true. My mama told me that as long as it's consenting it's OK. What those men did to you wasn't OK. You didn't consent." Tears fall from Aerial's eyes as she hugs Danyella. "What they did to all of you wasn't OK." Aerial's voice is muffled by Danyella's chest.

I step up behind them and bend down to be the same height as Aerial. I turn to her so she can see me, "No Hunny, it wasn't OK. Those were bad men. But these men," I motion to the prospects behind me, "You can trust. I trust them with my life and I hope you feel safe here. No one will ever hurt you again."

"I do. I trust them. They have kind eyes. The other men didn't. They were mean and their eyes were hard. Does that make sense?" Aerial darts a quick glance at the prospect behind us and then looks at me again.

"Yes, Aerial it does. It makes perfect sense. The eyes are the windows to the soul." I smile and rise to my feet.

"You two will be in here. Please take your time and we'll see you when you're done." I motion for Kensi and another girl to enter. They close the door behind them and lock it. The prospect stands idle in front of the door.

Danyella walks a few more feet to the third bathroom. "This is the last one. Same thing applies. Take your time and come back out the way you came when you're done. Monica and I will bring clothes for you." She twists the bathroom doorknob and opens it. The other two girls don't say a word and enter. They close and lock the door behind them and the final prospect stands at the door.

"Let's get some clothes. I'm sure between the club bunnies and us, we can find some." I suggest. Leading the way to the rooms at the far end, I open the door. This layout is different than the rest of the clubhouse. They bunk two or three to a room. It's designed like a college dorm. There are two beds on the right side of the room and another bed on the opposite. Three dressers and a walk-in closet are between the beds. I walk to the first dresser and open the drawer. Grabbing two packages of unopened underwear and two packages of socks. I close that drawer and open the next.

"If you two want to go to the next room and see what you can find, I'll meet you in a minute." I direct Danyella and Aerial.

"Is it safe? They won't have a fit if we're in the rooms?" Danyella asks.

I spin around, "Danyella. You have more authority over these women than anyone. Besides me, of course. You're the V.P.'s sister. If any of those bunnies have a problem with it, you come and find me. All these clothes are the property of the Royal Bastards. Not theirs. Anything with a Royal Bastards MC logo doesn't belong to them and I'll put each bitch in their place for giving you a hard time." Aerial releases a little giggle. "Fuck. I mean shit. I mean damn it. Ah hell, I give up. Aerial, I swear. I try not to but sometimes it happens."

"It's OK, Monica. My mama told me that sometimes people have to swear in order to get their point across. Or when they're really frustrated." Aerial smiles.

"Your mama sounds like a smart woman." I return her smile.

"She is. She's the best." Aerial turns her little face to Danyella. "Am I going to see her again?"

"Yeah, baby. You will real soon. Once Capone and the rest of the Royal Bastards get back, they'll help you ladies find your families." Danyella runs a hand down Aerial's face, soothing the stress lines away. "I promise. And for some reason we don't find your mama," Danyella bends down so she's looking directly at Aerial. "You will stay with me until we can find her. Does that sound like a deal?"

"Yes. Thank you, Dany." Aerial wraps her little arms around Danyella's neck and hugs her tight. They break apart and Danyella stands up.

"Come on cupcake, let's get some clothes." She takes Aerial's hand and together they leave the room.

I turn back around and rummage through the dresser drawers finding sweatpants, shorts, T-shirts and bras. Once I have a big pile of clothes, I go into the walk-in closet looking for something to carry all these clothes in. I flip the light switch and enter. I hate small spaces but it has to be done. I look upon the rows of shelves until I spot a suitcase up at the top in the back. I stretch on my tiptoes and use my fingertips to move it down. Once it drops, I bend down to pick it up. The hairs on the back of my neck stand on end, but I brush it off as being inside this tomb. Heavy footsteps alert me someone's in here. There should be no one here besides the brothers but my stomach sinks. My instincts are telling me I'm in trouble. I look in front of me and spot a baseball bat resting against the wall. I slowly move toward it, acting like I'm fixing the suitcase. I grab the bat with both hands, quickly. I turn and swing as hard as I can. The bat gives way into soft skin and a male oomph follows.

"What the hell, Monica?" Dagger cries with choppy breaths. He's holding his ribs with his left hand. "If you aimed higher, you would've cracked my skull wide open."

"Dagger? What the fuck are you sneaking up on me for?" I drop the bat and hurry over to him. "I'm so sorry. I heard footsteps and reacted." I help him sit on one of the beds. He's breathing better but still holding his ribs.

"You're vicious with that thing." He grunts in pain.

"I'm really sorry. What did you need?"

"To find my balls. I think they ran away when that bat came around." He releases a deep chuckle and I laugh with him. "Anyways. I wanted to let you know you can come see Daisy when you're done. She's stable. I'm not sure for how long though."

I look Dagger over from head to toe. He has blood all over his hands, arms, cut, T-shirt and jeans. Along with some on his rugged face. "Thank you. I'll be in soon. I appreciate you doing this. Saving her life."

"No worries." He pats my knee with a bloody hand and stands up. "Once I find my balls, I'll be in the room waiting for you to come see her." Dagger walks to the door and looks at me over his shoulder. "She's lucky to have someone like you on her side. It's not your fault."

"Thanks, Dagger." I give him a brittle smile and cast my eyes down onto the carpet. He doesn't understand it is my fault. I'm thankful for Dagger saving Daisy, but I don't know if I can see her. See the accusations in her eyes. Blaming me.

I stand up and grab the suitcase out of the closet, turning the light off and slamming the door shut behind me. I shove everything I can inside it and zip it up.

My phone vibrates in my back pocket and I pull it out. It's a text from Xander.

Xander: IDK if UR up but I'll be home soon. I need you.

Tears spring to my eyes. I need him and miss him so much even though it's only been a few hours. I need the comfort of his arms, the love in his eyes. The acceptance of the blood on my hands. I begin texting back but delete it. I do this a few more times before I decide on something simple. If he's distracted riding back here and something happens to him, that'd be another blame I'd have to shoulder. Who am I kidding? If something happens to Xander, I'd follow him wherever he went. Come hell or high water, I'll meet him in the afterlife. Together we will either be kicked out of heaven for creating chaos or condemned to hell for making the devil wish we weren't there.

Monica: I'll be here. I need you too.

Opening the door to the bedroom, I tuck my phone into my back pocket and run into Danyella and Aerial carting two suitcases full of clothes. We walk in silence to the first bathroom. I pull out the necessary clothes and knock on the door. Danyella does the same to the second bathroom. Once we have the clothes handed out, we make our way into the common room.

Dizziness overtakes me and I stumble. almost falling face-first onto the floor if Danyella didn't catch me. "What the hell Monica? Are you OK?"

"Yeah, I'm fine." I brush off her worried tone. "Just forgot where I was going." I head into the kitchen leaving Danyella and Aerial to sort out the girls.

The prospects are cooking up a feast and the scent of eggs, bacon, French toast, hash browns and sausage makes my stomach rumble. It's been all day since I've eaten anything. Must've been why I had that dizzy spell. I sneak a few pieces of bacon and wash it down with a bottle of water. I sit on the barstool at the five-foot-long white and blue marble island and wait for them to get done.

The kitchen is industrial size. A chef's dream come true. We have two thirty-six-inch stainless steel stoves against one wall with a cutting board in between them. Below them are two stainless steel ovens. To the right of the stoves is a double door stainless steel refrigerator. The island I'm sitting at has a sink made for washing your hands or washing vegetables. Behind me is another white and blue marble countertop and a dishwasher with a bigger stainless-steel sink. Cherry oak cupboards wrap around the space completing the whole kitchen.

"Monica, we're done. Where do you want all this food?" One prospect asks me.

"Let's set it up buffet style out in the common room on the bar. That way, the girls can eat as much as they want. I'll help." I hop down from the stool and another wave of dizziness washes over me. My ears ring and sweat beads on my brow. I shake it off and carry the dishes of food out. Once we have everything brought out and set up, Danyella tells the girls to come eat. I stand behind the bar watching everyone and eating some food of my own. Maybe it'll help with the dizziness. Some girls are relaxed and eating, laughing and joking around. Others are sitting quietly eating with their heads down. My guess is the girls who are the quietest have been there the longest. They've been brainwashed and they will be the hardest to integrate back into the real world. I wish there was something I could do to help them. To show them that even though evil does exist out there, good does too and it is possible to overcome the abuse they've endured.

My stomach rolls, threatening to bring everything back up I just ate. What the hell is wrong with me? I set my plate of mostly untouched food down and hurry into mine and Xander's room closing the door and locking it behind me. I need a minute to catch my bearing and let whatever's wrong with me pass.

I head into the bathroom and lean over the toilet. My stomach clenches and sweat beads on my forehead. After a few minutes nothing comes up and I feel a little better. With strength I didn't know I needed, I rise to my feet and stumble into the bedroom. My vision blurs and my heart is pounding hard against my chest. I think I need to lie down for a little while.

I fall onto the mattress. My arms and legs are numb. Footsteps outside the door has fear racing through my system. The hairs on the back of my neck stand on end. Someone's waiting on the other side of the door. I try to get my phone, but I can't move. I'm paralyzed.

The lock turns and the door opens slowly. Soft footsteps enter the room and the scent of lavender fills my nose. Panic sets in, I can't defend myself. I'm spiraling back to the past when Steam and Chains tortured me. Visions of that night send my heart into overdrive and I'm powerless to stop them.

"She's ready." I hear a female voice say before everything goes black.

Chapter 12

Blayze

With the howl of my tires on the pavement and the wind whipping through my helmet, Capone and I ride back to the clubhouse with our brothers right behind us. It was a successful night. We saved the girls and took down our rival club. It was pretty easy and that part worries me. My gut is telling me something isn't right. I crank the throttle, catching up to Capone. He looks over at me. His dark eyes are portraying what I'm feeling. He knows it was too easy. Capone signals with his left hand and we all pick up our speed. The tires of each bike eating up the distance between us and the clubhouse.

We reach the clubhouse in record time. Capone stops in front of the gate waiting for someone to let us in. Our bikes idling in the quiet night. The gate buzzes and rolls open. One by one we ride inside and head to the garage. The vans are still parked outside the entrance door. Krimson and her crew's cars are in the parking lot along with the Dodge Challenger Monica took. The garage door rolls up and we file inside. I park my bike next to Capone's and turn the key killing the motor. I remove my helmet, climb off my bike and head towards the common room, not waiting for anyone else. I want to see my girl and know she's OK. My boots echo down the marble corridor at a fast pace as the fluorescent lights kick on lighting up the path. My brothers will catch up eventually. Right now, my mind is set on getting to my girl.

I enter the common room and look around. There's a buffet style of food set up at the bar. Derange and a couple of prospects are standing next to it. Krimson and her crew are gathered near the pool tables talking in hushed tones. The girls we rescued are sitting anywhere they can, eating. Some are laughing and joking. Others are quiet with their heads down. I'm not seeing Monica. Danyella spots me standing in the doorway. A smile lights up her precious face. A face I never thought I'd see again. She sets her plate down and hurries over to me.

"Xander," Danyella hugs me tight. "Thank you for not giving up."

I return her embrace, "I'd never give up on my little sister. How are you holding up?"

"I'm OK. It'll take some time to adjust, but I think I'll be fine." She releases her hold on me and turns toward the others. "Some of them will be good, but I'm worried about a few. They were there the longest."

"I'm sure you'll be able to help them. You've always had a big heart." I put my hands on her shoulders giving them a little squeeze. "Listen, I want to talk to you, but I need to see Monica. Do you know where she is?"

"Are you two finally a thing now?" Danyella asks, raising an eyebrow.

"More than that. Have you seen her?" I smirk.

"It's about damn time." Danyella grins. "She was standing by the bar and then headed toward the bedrooms. My guess is she needed a break. She's been doing a lot and didn't look too good."

"Thanks." I kiss the top of Danyella's head and walk quickly toward my bedroom, not waiting for a response. I reach our bedroom door and twist the doorknob. The door swings open. Something isn't right. Monica would have locked the door behind her. She never enters a room without locking the door. It makes her feel safe since the attack.

I step inside and flip on the light switch. "Monica?" I shout into the room. No answer. "Monica?" I say again. Still no answer. I unholster my gun, looking around. The bed has an imprint on it where someone was laying down. Nothing else is out of place. I quietly walk into the bathroom. Nothing. I check the closet. Nothing. I look under the bed. Nothing.

Standing up, a light breeze flirts over my skin. The sheer curtains covering the window billow softly in the wind. Son of a bitch.

I hurry back to the common room with quick strides. Someone fucking took my girl, again.

"Capone!" I shout. All talking ceases as every set of eyes in the room land on me. You could hear a pin drop. "Capone!"

"Blayze, what's wrong?" Capone approaches me with his hands up.

"She's gone. She's fucking gone!" I'm a mess of emotions. The monster I've hidden away comes barreling back with a vengeance.

"OK, talk to me brother. Who's gone?" Capone doesn't raise his voice. He keeps it low and gentle like he's taming a wild animal.

"Monica. She's gone. Someone took her." My eyes scan the room, looking to see who's listening and who's guilty.

My brothers are surrounding us, making it impossible to see everyone. My chest is heaving with pent up rage and I'm about to explode.

"Church now!" Capone demands. He walks quickly into our sanctuary, I'm right behind him hot on his heels. Once the door clicks shut Capone slams the gavel onto the table with force. I'm surprised it didn't split in half. "What the fuck is going on?"

I'm too agitated to sit so I pace back and forth behind my chair. Running my hands through my hair, I yank on the ends trying to compose myself. "Danyella told me she saw Monica head into our room. She said Monica didn't look too good. So, I went there. She's gone, Capone. The window was open and she's not there. Someone took her."

"Are you sure?" Trigger asks from his seat. I give him a cold hard stare. Trigger raises his hands in defense. "I'm just asking."

"Yes, I'm fucking sure. The door was unlocked. Monica always locks the door behind her. It gives her peace of mind knowing she's safe behind a closed door since the attack." I grip the back of my chair hard. Rage is burning through my veins. "The fucking bedroom window is open. Motherfucker. She never opens it. And she isn't in there."

"Alright. Calm down." Capone raises his voice. If he wasn't my Prez I would've throttled him for telling me to calm down. "Who isn't here now that was before?" Capone looks at Dagger.

"I've been with Daisy saving her life. How in the fuck am I supposed to know?" Dagger growls.

"What about you, Bear?"

Bear shrugs his massive shoulders. "I've been keeping an eye on our prisoner. I didn't even realize you guys were back."

"That's it. Let me at him, Prez. He has answers." I need to get to the bottom of this.

"Aye. Red and Tiny go check the CCV cameras and see if you can find anything. Whoever did this knows the layout of our clubhouse. Dagger and Bear, stay with the girls. Watch for anything suspicious. The rest of you with Blayze and me." Capone slams the gavel on the table ending the meeting.

We all file out quickly heading to our designated spots. I'm walking at a fast pace toward the room where John fucking James is being held when a strong hand grips my shoulder, slowing me down. "I need you to keep a level head." Capone stares me down. "When I needed it, you put me in my place. Now I'm doing the same for you. We need answers and we won't get them if you kill him."

"I'm going to kill him but not until I get what we need. Trust me." I crack my neck.

"I do trust you. Right now, your head is ready to kill him. But trust what's in here." He jabs my stomach with his finger. "Trust this. I want my sister back but that won't happen if he's dead."

"Aye, Prez." I stop in front of the door separating me from the weasel dick motherfucker. "I won't kill him until I have answers."

Capone unlocks the door and I twist the knob, opening it. I step inside. John is tied to a metal chair in the middle of the floor. He picks his head up when he hears us enter. "It's about time you showed up. The hospitality sucks around here."

"Shut the fuck up." I circle around him. "You don't speak unless spoken to."

John tries to follow me, but his head will only swivel so far. I step around the chair until I'm towering over him. "Intimidation. I wouldn't expect anything less from you, Blayze." John says my name with disgust.

"Why were you working with Chains and the Bloody Scorpions?" I cross my arms over my chest. John casts his eyes down onto the floor not answering. "I'll ask you again because I know you're stupid. Why were you working with Chains?"

"Fuck off. I don't have to answer you."

"No, you don't. I can prolong your death and make you scream for your mama if you don't answer the question or I can make it quick if you tell me what you know." I lean over him and pull out my knife pressing it against his throat. "Either way you're not walking out of here."

"Fuck you, asshole."

"Fine." I nick his throat with the blade of my knife and blood trickles down onto his shirt. "Your choice." I split his shirt open with my knife exposing his skin. John struggles with the zip ties trying to get away. My fist connects with his ribs. A satisfying crunch vibrates up my arm. John inhales a sharp breath.

"Last chance, asshole. Why were you working with the Bloody Scorpions and who took Monica?" My fist connects with John's face and his head snaps back. Blood trickles from his nose.

His head snaps back. "Monica is missing?" The fear in his beady eyes is unmistakable.

"Yes, cock sucker. Someone took her." I hit him again in the ribs, hearing one crack under the force of my blow. "And you know who and why. So, tell me or that lung I just punctured will drown you and you'll die a slow and painful death."

I bring my fist back to punch him again. "Wait. Wait. Wait." John pleads trying to catch his breath.

I drop my fist, "I'm waiting." I growl.

"If someone took her from here then you have a rat. This thing is bigger than you know. I was only working for the Bloody Scorpions because they forced me. Made me do it. They found out about my fetish and used it against me. I swear I have nothing to do with Monica disappearing."

"You're full of shit." I press my blade against John's stomach and watch the blood seep out. I slowly pull my knife up, splitting the skin.

"I swear! I'm not lying!" John screams in pain. "The Bloody Scorpions were just a front for another club. Chains knew what he was doing when he approached them. Drew, my brother was a stupid idiot and fell for it. I didn't which is why they blackmailed me into using the studio to run the girls through." John clenches his jaw in pain. Sweat beads from his forehead. "I swear, Chains was using Drew and the rest of the MC. He knew they were your biggest rival and you wouldn't hesitate to take them down. Now with the Scorpions out of the way, there's room for one more. And if Monica is missing, the ball is already rolling." Tears fall down John's face mixing with his blood. "I don't know who it is, but if Monica is gone, she's in danger." He breathes harshly, trying to catch his breath through the punctured lung. I should feel bad, but I don't.

John James brought this on himself. He knew the moment he crossed us this would be the end. "Just do it. End me now. But promise me you'll find her. She might not have loved me, but I did care for her."

Adrenaline fuels my body. My hand is steady as I drive the blade into John's throat ending his life. No one in the room says a word as the life drains from John James's eyes. Once his body stops twitching, I drag my eyes from his limp form and land on Capone.

"Let's go brother and sniff out a rat." Capone walks out the door and I follow. We have a traitor among our ranks and we won't stop until he's found.

Chapter 13

Blayze

I'm pacing back and forth in the common room waiting to hear from Tiny and Red. They've been holed up in the communications room poring over the CCV cameras for the last hour. One of the prospects and Dagger cleaned up John James' body and disposed of it. We don't know who to trust so each prospect will always have a patched in club member with them until this is resolved.

The girls we brought in are still up. Some are wandering around the room while others are sleeping on the couches and chairs. They've had a hard life and deserve to be at peace even if it's temporary.

Danyella approaches me sitting at the bar. Her once vibrant green eyes are haunted. Her skinny frame makes me agitated all over again. "Hey big brother."

"Hey, squirt. How are you doing?" I turn to face Danyella as she sits next to me on the other stool. I feel bad for not asking her what happened when we got back but finding Monica has been my top priority.

"I've been worse." She shrugs her shoulders. "Want to tell me what's going on? I know Monica is missing and you're sitting here like a wounded puppy."

I bark out a laugh spinning the beer bottle between my fingers. I haven't taken a drink, but I really want to. "Well, you nailed it. Someone took her and we don't know who yet. Once we find out though, everything is off the table."

"Xander, please be careful. These men, they have no code. No ethics. No brotherhood. They don't care who they hurt or why. It's how they got me." Danyella rests her hand on my arm, drawing my attention.

"How did they get you?" I should've asked this earlier and now I'm a piece of shit brother who was more concerned about his girlfriend than his sister.

"Don't beat yourself up, Xander." Danyella puts a little bit of pressure on my arm. "I was walking down the street when a van pulled up right alongside me. It was broad daylight and I didn't think someone would dare touch me." She stares off into space replaying what happened in her mind. "I mean come on, you're my brother. Who in their right mind would touch a Royal Bastards sibling? Well, they did. They took me right off the street, put a bag over my head, bounded my hands and feet so I couldn't fight back. Trust me I tried." Danyella tucks a piece of her blonde hair behind her ear.

"Did they say anything?"

"Just that being Blayze's sister, I'll bring in a lot of money when the time came. There's one thing that doesn't add up though."

I turn to face Danyella and wrap my arms around her. "You're safe here, squirt."

"I know. But I need to tell you this. The men who took me and the men who held me hostage weren't…"

Tiny and Red open the door interrupting Danyella. "Capone! Blayze! We got something."

"Hold that thought, Danyella. I'll be right back." I hurry over to them with Capone right on my heels. "What did you find?" I'm searching the cameras they have playing.

Red speaks first. "It took us a while to find it because they avoided the cameras at all costs. But she did make one mistake." Red hits play and the screen comes to life.

"She? What do you mean she? Our kidnapper is a woman?" I ask.

"Just watch," Red replies.

My eyes are glued to the screen when a woman in a black hoodie approaches the camera and pulls the hood off her head. The purple streaks in her hair are unmistakable. She flips us off and runs toward the back of the gym. Samantha, the club bitch.

"Son of a bitch! I'm going to kill her." Capone growls. He's out the door before anyone can say anything.

I hurry after him and head to the back of the gym. It's still night out and the floodlights don't reach back here. I pull my phone from my pocket and turn on the flashlight app. The fence butts up to the back of the building with only a small space to fit through and goes higher than the building's roof. Capone and I search all around the fence and don't see how they got in and out.

"The motherfucker from Los Demons. How'd he get through the fence?" I speak out loud. I look up and down, not seeing how they were able to pull this off. "The only way in and out is through the gates. So, how'd they do it?"

Capone takes off into the building leaving me standing here. I hear shuffling feet above me and shine my flashlight toward the noise. Capone comes into view at the rooftop. "Son of a bitch. I figured it out. Blayze get up here now."

I hurry around the side of the building, into the gym doors and head up the stairs that lead to the roof. My footsteps echo along the hallway. I shoulder the door open and search for Capone. He's standing at the edge of the roof staring out into the darkness.

"What'd you find?"

"Look," Capone points to the edge of the roof toward the fence. I shine my flashlight in that direction and see what he sees. They cut the fence that towers over the building. Small enough for a person to fit through but not big enough for us to see from below. "My guess is that they cut this part of the fence, had a ladder on the other side and used it to get in and out."

"What the fuck? How'd they avoid the cameras set up all over the clubhouse? And how'd they get Monica out without her causing a scene?" I'm beyond pissed off now.

"That I'm not sure about. But if Samantha was behind this, she knew where the cameras were set up at. She knows our blind spots and the ins and outs of the clubhouse. I'm going to fucking kill her when I get my hands on her." Capone turns on his boots and walks back into the gym. Leaving me up here by myself.

I squat down and stare into the darkness. The city of angels lights up the view far away in the distance. "Where are you Bug? Give me something here."

"Blayze?" Danyella approaches me and stares out into the darkness. I rise to my feet and wrap an arm around my sister's shoulders. "I'm so sorry this happened. What can I do to help?"

"Tell me everything you can about the men who took you. Leave out no details. It might be the only way we can catch these fuckers." I peer into Danyella's green eyes. Pain and turmoil swirl in her once vibrate and cheerful gaze.

"Ok. But not up here. This is going to take a while," she whispers softly.

I offer Danyella my hand and she takes it squeezing it for comfort. "Come on then. Let's head back to the clubhouse and get Capone. Maybe hearing what happened will help us track Monica down." Together we leave the roof and head into the clubhouse. I find Capone in his room pacing back and forth.

"Danyella is going to tell us everything that happened while she was kidnapped," I explain to Capone. Danyella and I enter and she sits on his bed.

Capone sits next to her and gently takes her hand in his. "Take your time. It's just the three of us and anything you say will stay between us."

"Thank you," Danyella offers Capone a sad smile.

Chapter 14

Danyella

My heart is pounding hard against my chest when Capone grabs my hand and squeezes it affectionately. I've always had a crush on this strong, loveable but asshole man. I've never acted on any of my feelings and then I was taken away from him and my brother. I never thought we'd be sitting here shoulder to shoulder, hand in hand. But we are. And they're waiting for me to tell them what happened.

I inhale a deep breath and steady my nerves. "I don't like to think about what happened to me. I tried the whole, ignore it and it'll go away thing, but every day when I woke up chained to the bed, I knew I couldn't ignore it. When my body would be sore from the beatings, I couldn't ignore it. And now Monica needs me so I can't ignore it."

"Take your time, Danyella." Capone's smooth voice and warm hands soothe me.

"As I told Xander earlier, they took me right off the street in broad daylight. I tried to fight them off but there were so many of them and one of me. I was targeted for a reason. These men threw a bag over my head and zip-tied my hands and feet."

Leaving this little boutique store in the heart of L.A., I catch a glimpse of a black van following me down the street. There are people all around me and I'm the sister of the V.P. of the Royal Bastards MC. There is no way someone would mess with me. Not in broad daylight. Not on a busy street.

I continue to walk with my head held high, not letting them know I know they're there. I don't know who they are or why they're after me, so I pick up my pace and walk faster. Once I reach the end of the street, I step out into traffic trying to lose the van. Horns blare and I'm forced to step back when a car almost clips me. With a racing heart, I look around to see if the van is still here, but they sped away.

I continue down the street when the traffic allows and walk into the parking garage where I left my car. The hair on the back of my neck stands on end. I remove my keys from my jeans pocket and hold them tight in my fist like Xander taught me. If these jerks come back, I'll stab them with my keys.

Screeching tires echo through the parking garage causing me to jump. I look around but no one is here. It's just me. I need to stop being so jumpy. No one will attack me. I hurry my stride, my feet slap against the concrete making an echoing noise. I see my car in the distance and break out into a run. Tires screech again in the distance.

I get closer to my car and hit the key fob nestled safely in my hand. The horn beeps, letting me know the doors are unlocked. I release a shaky breath and relax. I reach my car and open the door. A sharp pain explodes from the back of my head and I'm thrown against the door and the frame of my car. I turn around to see who's behind me when a bag is thrown over my head. I kick and scream, fighting with everything I have. I dropped my keys in the scuffle. I keep on fighting, not giving up so easily when a fist connects with the side of my covered head, stunning me.

Hands grip my shoulders and feet as I'm being carried away. I kick and wiggle my body making it hard for whoever has me to carry me away. My foot breaks free from their hold and I slam it into a body.

"You little bitch. You're going to pay for that one," a man's voice growls in my ear. Hot rancid breath enters the bag as whoever's holding my shoulders whispers. I stifle a gag and fight their hold on me. I slip free but only for a moment. I can't see where I'm going or get the bag off my head quick enough to get away. A fist hits me again in the face and white spots bloom from the blow. Punches and kicks rain down onto me until I'm completely immobile. Pain shoots through my face and body as hands grab for me again.

"Tie her fucking feet and throw her in the van," a man barks. "She's going to bring us a lot of money."

I'm in so much pain I can't hear the rest of what they're saying. Hands grab me again and I try to fight but they're stronger than I am. My hands are bound behind my back and my feet are bound tightly. I don't have the energy to fight back. I'm lifted and tossed like a rag doll onto cold unyielding steel. I hit my head hard when I land leaving me dizzy.

"Get her to the Prez. And if she comes too, knock her ass out again." The same man says. A door slams and I'm moving. I wiggle a little bit, trying to see how tight the restraints are but my shoulders are on fire and my face and body aches.

"Don't fucking move or I'll kill you," another male voice says to my right. I try to move my head in his direction but the vehicle turns a corner and I'm thrown to the other side, slamming my head against the side. Dizziness takes hold and I stifle the vomit trying to make its way up my throat.

"Why are you doing this?" I whisper.

I'm not expecting an answer, but I get one. "That's for us to know and you to find out soon, Danyella." The way he says my name sends a chill down my spine. These men will hurt me if I can't escape. "Don't even think about it, bitch. You have nowhere to go and no one will save you."

"Blayze," I mumble through the bag. "He'll save me."

The man barks out a laugh, "If you think that pussy will save you, you're in for a big surprise. The Royal Bastards are scum. They won't care that you're missing. They only care about themselves. You're in hell little girl, get used to it."

I sob and curl up into a ball the best I can. They're wrong. They're so wrong. Blayze will find me and when he does all these jerks are dead.

I must've fallen asleep during the ride because the van brakes hard and I roll to the opposite side. A groan escapes my lips. I have to figure out how to get out of here. The back doors open and strong hands grip my feet, pulling me towards them. I kick and fight through the pain in my body, desperate to get away. A fist lands in my stomach causing the breath to escape my lungs. Damn, that hurts.

"Stop fighting and it'll go easier for you," the man that rode in the back with me growls.

"Never. I'll never stop fighting you."

"We've got a feisty one. She'll be fun," another voice says and the blood running through my veins freeze. I know that voice.

He stuns me long enough for them to grab my legs and yank me the rest of the way out of the van. I'm thrown over a bony shoulder and pain shoots through my stomach. I kick my feet but don't come into contact with anything. A hand grips my hair though the hood and tears spring in my eyes as the hairs are ripped from my head.

"Stop it little bitch or I'll have to hurt you." I wish I can see who these men are. "You're stuck with us and if you don't fight, my boys won't hurt you. They like it rough."

"What do you want from me?" I ask.

"You'll find out soon enough. Now shut the fuck up before my brother has a go at your precious ass." He releases my hair and I don't fight. Fear freezes me. I'm too drained to try again right now.

I hear traffic in the distance when a door opens and slams shut behind us. The man carrying me over his shoulder jars my stomach as he takes quick steps. I can tell we're going down and not up. That means I'm heading toward a basement of some sort. My heart slams against my chest when we reach the bottom stairs. The man carrying me is panting by the time we stop. No one says a word when I hear another door open. I'm trying to come up with a plan to get the hell out of here but the further we walk, the more reality sets in. I can't escape.

The stench hits me through the bag before anything else. It's a nasty smell of pee and poop being stifled in a room. I hold back a gag. The last thing I want is to throw up and have it crusted around my face.

A loud metal rattle causes me to jump. Sniffling and crying pierce the room we're in. When a man speaks. "Wake up, bitches. I have another one for you." A loud slam of metal against metal makes me jump and I start kicking again.

"No! You can't do this. I've done nothing wrong." I cry and kick and fight with everything I have.

"Hold her fucking feet, now." The man in charge growls. Someone grabs my feet with a strong grip and I'm being lifted off the shoulder of the man carrying me. I'm dizzy from the sudden movement and slammed into a wall. My head bounces off the unforgiving concrete and the air rushes out of my lungs on impact. The bag is yanked off my head and I blink a few times. I'm surrounded by four men wearing cuts. Each states their rank but no road name. What the hell?

"Oh shit." The words tumble out of my mouth before I can stop them.

"That's right little bitch. Oh shit. You're at my mercy now." He bends down so his face is right next to my ear. "If you try anything, I will fuck you up. Then I'll let him," he motions to another man standing behind us, "have his way with you. He likes the fighters." The man he's talking about smirks and adjusts himself.

"Why are you doing this? What has my brother done to you?" I plead for an answer. When one doesn't come, I lean my head back against the wall and blow out a breath of frustration.

The man stands up and grabs my feet, dragging me across the floor. My shoulders and arms burn and I have nothing to grab ahold of to stop myself from going. He yanks me up and plops me down onto a bed in the corner of the room. The zip ties are cut and I move my arms, trying to swing but I'm not fast enough. My one hand is cuffed to the wall, stretched beyond normal.

"Now, if you're a good girl we'll leave you alone. If you continue to be a pain in my ass, I'll break you." The man in charge growls.

"You still didn't answer me. Can you please tell me why you're doing this and who are you?" I plead with tears in my eyes.

"Let's just say your brother owes me. The whole MC owes me and the only way to make them suffer is through you. You're just an unlucky bitch caught up in a war." He glances around the room before his brown eyes land back on me. *"And the Los Demons take no mercy."*

A gasp leaves my lips. Oh, this is bad. This is really, really bad. Los Demons are a horrific MC. They've been known for human trafficking. Girls enter their clubhouse never to be seen again and I ended up in the middle of it.

I glance around the room and see around twenty women down here. Some are watching us and others have their backs to us like they've given up hope. Each has their own cot and one of their wrists is cuffed above their heads. There is no way out of this. Fighting just causes them to get pissed off and hurt me. Crying does nothing for the psychopaths. I have to stay strong and pray Blayze will find me before they either kill me or sell me.

Chapter 15

Blayze

I can't take my baby sister telling me anymore right now. I know I have to, but my heart is shattering with every word she speaks. Every tear she sheds, every shudder that passes through her body. The Los Demons beat her, raped her and broke her so badly she almost gave up hope. My blood is boiling thinking about them hurting her like they did. Violating her body, shattering her mind, abusing her soul. I will rip each and every one of them apart with my bare hands. I'm going to fuck them up so badly, their mamas won't be able to identify their bodies.

"I was so close to ending my life. That was until Aerial and Daisy came." Danyella has silent tears rolling down her cheeks. "They needed me just as much as I needed them. Together the three of us helped each other. When one of us was suffering, the others would be there. We grew a bond and it pissed some of the other girls off. Then Daisy disappeared." Danyella's voice is full of pain and despair.

"That must've been when we found her." I clench my fists on my thighs thinking about what that weasel dick fuckface was doing to her. What the Los Demons could be doing to Monica right now. "Did they take you anywhere? Anywhere you might remember?"

Danyella wipes the tears from her face and squeezes Capone's hand. Her eyes widen, "Yes. They would always put a bag over my head and bound my feet and hands when transporting me. But one time they didn't. One time we walked down the street. Me, Aerial and a member of the Bloody Scorpions. It was right before Monica rescued me."

"Where did you go?" Capone asks through clenched teeth. The tick in his jaw is visible. He's seething with rage.

"We went to a strip club down the street. In the back, there's a secret room where they took a picture of me and Aerial. I remember the Bloody Scorpion telling a member of Los Demons something about the two of us making them a lot of money. That there will be top dollar paid for the little girl and because I was a family member of the Royal Bastards that enemies you guys have will run the bids up so high, they'll be swimming in cash."

I look at Capone with fury in my eyes. We've got a lead. He nods his head once and I'm out of my chair. I approach Danyella and cup her precious face in my hands. "I'm so sorry you went through that because of us. Because of me. I swear we will make this right." I hug my baby sister tight, hoping that she can get past the abuse she endured, giving her some of my strength to fight through the dark days.

"It's not your fault, Xander." Danyella cries against my shoulder. Her tears seeping into my cut. She wraps her arms around my waist holding me tight. "If anything, it was their choice to do what they did. I'm grateful for you shutting them down and rescuing me. Now, go find Monica, she's in danger." Danyella squeezes my waist one last time before releasing me.

I turn and walk out the door, taking one last glance at my sister. She's silently crying while Capone holds onto her, giving her strength. Capone looks up at me with cold black eyes. He wants revenge just as much as I do. We're going to get revenge on every single Los Demons and the little bitch working with them.

I walk down the hallway and into the common room. Most of the girls are sleeping on makeshift beds scattered across the room. Krimson and her crew are still here, they're all sitting at the bar watching over the girls with concern. I approach them and Krimson and her boyfriend Nolan turn in my direction.

"What's going on?" Krimson asks. Her honey-colored eyes and sultry voice sends a chill down my spine every time she speaks. I imagine she has the same effect on every other male in the United States.

"We have a lead. Danyella just told Capone and me where they took her right before Monica rescued her. I'm riding to check it out." I contain the rage pouring through my blood long enough to speak, but it's hard. I want to rip their heads off and spit down their throats. "And it wasn't just Blood Scorpions. They were a front being used by Los Demons."

"Los Demons? Are you sure?" Krimson asks. She stands quickly and paces back and forth. "That can't be right. Los Demons have been on the down-low for quite some time. Not even showing their faces or cuts in the city. I would've known."

"Obviously they pulled one over on you too. They have a strip club near the warehouse where they kept the girls." I'm pissed the fuck off that Krimson thinks Danyella is lying. "My sister wouldn't lie about this shit. Not after what she fucking told me."

"Hold on a second, Blayze. Going there will tip them off. We need to play this one smart." Krimson whisper shouts so she doesn't wake up the girls.

"I won't hold on," I roar. Fuck the ones sleeping. I've lost all rational thought when she told me to hold on. "If you heard what those pencil dick motherfuckers did to my sister and then had the only person you've ever loved drugged and kidnapped, you'd be ready to rip some heads off too."

"I get it, I do." Krimson takes a step putting her right in my face. "But if you go in there now, they'll kill Monica the moment they hear your bike rumble down the street. Let me send two of my crew in. Have them scope the place out."

"That could work," Capone says from behind me. I turn to look at my Prez. He has murder in his black eyes. "But I'll only give you an hour. Then we're coming in and gutting each and every person in that club."

"Fine. I can work with an hour." Krimson turns and walks toward the Latino chick sitting at the bar. I think her name is Hotflash. They whisper back and forth, Hotflash's hands fly up and down as she speaks. Then she leaves with a dark-haired man with blonde highlights trailing behind her. "Hotflash and Rush are heading there now. They'll report back to me as soon as they have something. Wait! Where are you going?" Krimson is right behind Capone and me as we head into the garage.

"We're heading out and waiting around the corner. I'm not staying here when I can be there." Capone gruffly replies. "If you knew what they did to Danyella, you'd be doing the same thing." Capone passes Bear, Tiny, Derange, Trigger, Red, Torch and Dagger. They all follow us into the garage with Krimson and her crew right on our heels.

"You keep saying that but nothing else. What the hell Capone. Tell me what I'm getting my crew into." Krimson shouts grabbing Capone's arm, stopping us all in our tracks. Capone turns around and pins Krimson with a glare so deadly, I fucking hide my balls.

"You want to know what that girl currently in my bedroom went through?" Capone shrugs off Krimson's hold on his arm and gets in her face. Her boyfriend Nolan releases a low growl, but that doesn't stop Capone. "If I tell you how they beat her, raped her and abused her daily, will that help you sleep at night if you follow through with us and end them? If you see the scars marring her body, if you see her tortured soul battling with the darkness trying to take over, will that help you in your decision? If you see the one person I've ever cared about struggle to stay alive and live again, will that help solidify your decision?" Capone roars so loud the walls shake. His body is vibrating with rage and the darkness is taking over his mind. "If you hear the story of how she was tortured and raped six times in one day to the point where she couldn't fight back anymore, will that make you happy Krimson?"

Krimson releases a shaky breath and shakes her head. "No. Come on, what are we waiting for?" She disappears outside along with the rest of her crew.

I glare at Capone and he stares back at me, daring me to say something. "My baby sister huh?" That's all I can come up with at the moment. I'm stunned speechless for the first time ever.

"We'll talk about it later. Right now, we have to save my sister." Capone straddles his bike and throws his helmet on. The rest of us do the same. We fire up our bikes and roll out of the garage. Once we're outside the security gate a prospect opened, Capone opens up his beast of a bike and we ride into the darkness.

I keep replaying what Capone said in my mind. How Danyella was the only woman he's ever cared about. Now that he confessed, even out of anger, I see the signs. Since she disappeared, he was more active in screwing the club bunnies. Or letting them suck him off, but I've never seen him show any type of attachment to any of them. They were just a hole to fill the void of missing Danyella. I'm such an inconsiderate jackass. I should've known, but I was so lost in my own despair, I missed it. I was so infused with my own issues I missed my best friend's struggle.

Capone revs his bike pulling me out of my head. He signals to turn right and we follow. Eight bikes and six cars park in a parking lot about a mile away from the Los Demons strip club. I kill the engine and set my boots on the concrete. I hold my bike up with the power in my thighs and light up a cigarette. Capone puts his kickstand down and climbs off his bike, heading right for me.

"Ready?" He asks when he gets closer.

"Ready, Prez. Are we sure about this?" I want to make sure he isn't just going in there to murder a bunch of people out of rage. That his head is leading the game, not his heart.

"As sure as I'll ever be." Capone lights up a cigarette, inhaling the smoke and letting it go. "Danyella told me she knew for sure they would keep Monica there. When we took out the Bloody Scorpions and their hideouts, Los Demons would keep Monica near the auction site. She said girls would go to the strip club and not come back. She learned to keep her mouth shut and her ears open."

"I wish she never went through this," I grumble, stubbing out my cigarette.

"Me too, brother." Capone rests a hand on my shoulder giving it a tight squeeze. "And I wish it didn't take

Danyella being kidnapped for me to know how I really felt about her. Now that I've admitted it to myself, I can't stop thinking about what I'm going to do to these fuckers."

"Me too. If they've harmed Monica the way they did Danyella, I'm going to lose my shit. No woman should go through what Danyella did. No woman should be abused and mistreated the way she was." Anger and rage are vibrating through my body. Capone releases my shoulder and straightens his spine. A car pulls into the parking lot at a high speed, tires squealing on the concrete. I put my kickstand down and hurry over to Krimson's car where they stopped. Hotflash and Rush step out of the car.

"They have her there," Hotflash mutters and a shiver runs down my spine.

"What else?" Krimson asks, leaning against the hood of her car.

Hotflash's dark eyes find mine and she inhales a sharp breath before continuing. "Their whole MC is there. It was a creepy vibe the moment we walked in the door. Women were dancing but the men weren't paying attention to them like they were putting on a front for onlookers. They were all on edge, watching the door. Rush and I had to play it off as if I was a dancer looking to get hired or they would've kicked us out in an instant."

"Did you see my sister?" Capone asks trying to hurry Hotflash along.

"Hotflash tried to get into the back room, but it's being guarded. I'm not sure how you're going to get in there without getting killed. They're all strapped with guns on high alert." Rush finishes.

"Let us handle that," Capone speaks. He turns his head to Krimson, "I understand if you want to stay here,

Krimson. This will get messy and there will be blood on our hands. You don't need that on your crew either."

"I'm in. It's up to them if they want in on it. No one fucks with my town and gets away with it." Krimson stands tall and looks at every member of her crew. No one says they won't go. "It's settled then. We're with you."

"Wait," Nolan speaks for the first time since I met him. "This is what my guys and I do. Let us help." He walks to the back of a car, pops the trunk and pulls out two black bags. He brings them to the front of Krimson's car and opens them. "Take these and we can communicate back and forth." He hands us tiny earpieces and I put mine in. Nolan then hands each of his men an AK-47 and a .40 caliber handgun with extra ammo.

"Prez," Red shouts grabbing Capone's attention while running our way. "There are two other ways in. One from the rooftop and a backdoor. The blueprints of the building were just sent to my phone."

Capone grabs Red's phone and hands it to Nolan. "What's the best way?"

Nolan studies the blueprints for a few minutes. "If here was guarded like Hotflash said," he points to a room in the back. "There's only one way in and out. We keep two men at the front entrance and two at the back. The rest of us climb up the fire escape and use the roof. They won't expect us to come in that way. Once we get in, the two in the front need to create a diversion and draw them all away. Then we move fast. Take out any members in our way. Capone and Blayze, you stay with me, Krimson and Ashton. The four of us will move quickly to the back room and get Monica out."

"Tiny and one of your men will take the back. Torch and another will take the front and create the diversion." Capone responds. "Trigger, Dagger, Bear,

Derange and the rest of your crew will take out the main room while we go into the back and get my sister." Capone looks at every member of his MC. "Does anyone have any issues with this?"

"We're good, Prez," I answer when no one responds.

"Good," Capone hands Red's phone back to him. "Let's roll out. It's time for war boys. Have no mercy. Take no prisoners. You have the green light to kill on sight. Our cleanup crew will handle the rest."

I quickly stride over to my bike and throw my leg over it. Firing it up, I let the roar of my beast settle in my bones. It's time for battle. There will be bloodshed. There will be death. There will be no mercy.

Chapter 16

Monica

Darkness surrounds me. I'm running as fast as my legs will take me through the woods. My lungs are burning from lack of oxygen. My thighs are screaming in pain. But I can't stop. I won't stop. Twigs and branches swat me in the face. Weeds reach for my ankles tripping me and I fall hard. I throw my hands up to protect my face. Pain shoots through my right wrist. I roll over onto the dirt facing the dark sky trying to catch my breath. Stars twinkle against the inky black night.

Heavy footsteps crunch against the fallen leaves. Closer and closer, the familiar ragged breathing that haunts my dreams approaches me. They've found me. He's found me, again. I try to stand but pain shoots through my ankle causing me to fall back down stifling a scream trying to rip from my throat.

"Little bitch, I can hear you. I'm coming for you," Chains' deep voice echoes through the forest.

My heart hammers against my chest, sweat beads on my brow. I crawl through the dirt and leaves trying to hide against the side of a wide oak tree. My biggest fear is coming to life. I lean against it and close my eyes for a moment, trying to steady my rapid heartbeat and even my breathing.

I sense him before I see him. Chains has always been larger than life in my mind. His tormenting voice reaches me before he does sending a chill down my spine. "You know I always find you. I'll always find you. You're mine to own, my possession."

I try to move but my body isn't cooperating with my head. My brain is screaming at me to keep moving, but my body has given up, shutting down. Chains grabs my hair from around the tree and yanks hard smashing my head against the hard oak. I feel pieces of it being ripped from my scalp. Dizziness causes my head to swim.

I scream in pain.

"Got you, little bitch. You can't get away from me, ever." Chains' rancid breath streams across my face and I stifle a gag. "No matter where that fucking worthless brother tries to hide you, I will find you." Chains yanks my hair again and I'm falling.

I hit my head on the wooden floor.

I look around through tear-filled eyes and instead of being in the forest, I'm in my bedroom in my old apartment in Detroit. Punches rain down onto my face, I curl into a ball, trying to stop the steel-toed kicks to my stomach. New pain from the beating he and Steam just delivered onto me burns through my body. Chains flips me over and straddles my waist with his heavy body. He leans down so his face is inches from mine. The hardness in his jeans makes me gag.

"You know I like it when you fight back, little bitch." Chains grip my bruised face with his fingers squeezing hard enough to make me whimper.

"What do you want?" I ask through the pain.

"You."

That one word has me quivering in fear. I will not go down like this. I will not let this asshole take something from me that was never his to begin with. I buck my hips trying to throw him off, but he's so much heavier than me. Chains laughs deep in his throat and moves so his legs are straddling the top of my thighs. He gropes my chest with blood coated fingers, my blood, and squeezes my nipple hard enough I cry out in pain.

Flashbacks of my childhood come rearing back. The first time he pinched my ass and said it was an accident. The first time his hand touched my growing breasts and said it was a mistake. The look of want and lust radiating from Chains' eyes. Capone saw him touch me inappropriately one day and he lost it. He beat the hell out of Chains and that's what started the war within the Club. It was all my fault. Everything that's happened right up to this moment was my fault.

I stare into Chains' cold dead eyes and laugh. Blood drips from my mouth. I've lost my mind. "You can't take something that's not there anymore Chains." I spit out his name and watch the coldness change to fury. "It's not yours to take and you can thank Blayze for that one." I laugh maniacally. "It was a goodbye fuck and guess what Chains? It was in your bed. My big fuck you to you!" It's not true, we actually did it in Blayze's room the night before I left, but I want to torment Chains the way he's torturing me.

Chains' fingers squeeze my throat cutting off my air. My vision blurs but I'm still smirking through blood-stained lips. He's losing control. Chains releases my throat and I inhale gulps of air. "Is that all you got?"

"Fucking whore, just like your mother," Chains roars against the side of my head and leans back. He wraps his free hand around my throat again and squeezes slightly.

"The difference," I say through clenched teeth, "is that she fucked you and I'd rather die than have your disease infested dick anywhere near my pussy."

The fury in his cold dead eyes is unmistakable, Chains' body is vibrating with rage. A smirk appears across his rugged face. "Little girl, don't you know I hold all the cards?" He pulls out a long jagged knife from his cut and holds it under my nose. "I'll make you wish you were dead, then I'll haunt you for the rest of your life. I'm the shit nightmares are made of."

Chains moves the knife down my throat nicking it as he goes. A small trickle of blood streams down my neck and over his fingers still gripping my throat. He drags the cold steel against my shirt and it rips away like butter. He glides the knife down my torso, nicking my skin as he goes.

"There's one thing I hold the power to. One thing you want more than anything and I'm taking it." Chains sinks the knife into my stomach and white-hot pain radiates through my body. He pulls it out and does it again, repeatedly. I scream but Steam, the president of Savage Saints, Detroit, covers my mouth so my screams are stifled. My blood flows freely from my body as Chains brutalizes me. His heavy panting is something I'll never forget.

Suddenly Chains' weight is lifted from my body and I can move. Only I've lost so much blood and I'm in so much pain, all I can do is lay there. I can't fight back. I blackout as heavy footsteps scrap across the floor, getting further and further away.

Jolting awake in the chair I've been tied to, I blink a few times before realizing where I am. It was just a dream. The nightmare that plagues me every moment I try to sleep. Reliving what Chains did to me always sends my mood into a dark place. A place I can't escape. My body is trembling from fear. He's dead. He can't hurt me anymore.

"You're finally awake. Did the princess get her beauty sleep?" A female voice full of venom and hatred comes from the shadows behind me. It sounds familiar, but she's hiding from me and has been since I've been tied to this chair.

"Show me your face," I demand.

Laughter rings through the small room I'm being held in. I can hear the bass of music coming from the other side of the door, vibrating my body. I still haven't figured out where I am, but the smell of sweat and sex is thick in the air.

"Where am I and how did you get me here? Who the fuck are you?"

"Still a demanding little bitch, aren't you? This is all your fault you know." She moves in the shadows behind me. Staying just out of sight. "If you didn't come back, you wouldn't be here right now. The Royal Bastards wouldn't have had a rat in the ranks and Blayze wouldn't feel the ultimate betrayal."

The scent of lavender fills my nose. It's nagging in the back of my mind because it's so familiar, but I can't quite place it. Suddenly my head is being yanked back, the hair being pulled from the roots. All thoughts leave my mind as my fight or flight instincts kick in. Just coming off that horrible nightmare, I'm slow to respond but a groan slips past my throat and I tighten my body.

I try to fight back but I can't move my hands or legs. I shake my head trying to get her grip off my hair. A hard slap sends my head reeling to the side. Blood falls from my lips. Just like in my dream.

"What do you want from me?"

"I want you gone so I can claim my rightful place." Her lips are right at my ear whispering.

I turn my head and come face to face with the woman who's holding me hostage. My eyes widen in surprise. "Samantha?" She's pulled her purple streaked blonde hair up in a ponytail. No make-up on and bruises surround her throat. She isn't wearing our club colors, thank God, but she is wearing a Los Demons t-shirt and leather pants with her six-inch stiletto heels. Her blue eyes are full of rage. I suddenly have a dark urge to stick that fake ass heel into her fake ass face.

"You're not stupid after all are ya?" She smirks, yanking my head back. I blink through the tears swelling in my eyes from the pain.

"Why? After we took you in, gave you a place to live, clothes on your back and a roof over your head. Why would you do this to the club that gave you everything?"

"Gave me everything?" Samantha's maniacal laughter rings through the small room. "Your club took everything from me. My life, my youth, my love. You took everything from me."

"How? How did I take anything from you?" I'm really confused on what her crazy bitch-ass is talking about.

Before she can answer, the door opens letting the music from the other room in with them. The noise is loud and annoying before the door slams shut. Heavy footsteps scrape across the wooden floor. Each step comes closer toward us. I watch Samantha's face turn from cold hard rage to the fake ass sweet smile she saves for men she wants to fuck. I've seen her give that look to both Capone and Blayze numerous times. The bitch is going down.

Samantha releases her claws from my hair and shoves my head forward. She walks around the room with her hands clasped in front of her. Around and around she goes. The man who entered is watching her every move. He has on a Los Demons cut but his back is to me so I can't see his face. Fucking chicken shit. I watch both of them while trying to free my hands from the ropes. My skin burns raw, but I don't stop. I can't quit now.

"When I came to the club it wasn't by choice." Samantha's voice takes on a low quiet vibe. "I was forced to go by my slut of a mother. She got involved with Chains. She was one of his many side pieces." Samantha stares off into space lost in her own head. "She never believed me when I told her what he was doing to me. She laughed it off and said he'd never touch a dirty little girl like me. Only thing was, he did. For years, I suffered from his abuse, his leering looks. I saw him do the same to you, only you had Capone and Blayze to stand up for you while I was left by myself to suffer the abuse alone. I really thought you and I would become friends from what he did to both of us, but you were so self-centered that you didn't see me." Samantha spins on her heels, pieces of her purple streaked hair whips around her face. "You didn't see me. But you see me now. And when I'm finished with you, Blayze will see me too."

"Are you finished yet?" The low raspy voice of the Los Demon's member speaks to Samantha.

"Almost. I was just getting to the good part." Samantha turns to the man and flashes him a sexy smile. I see through it. I see the hurt and pain behind that smile and I want to help. The only thing is, she doesn't want my help. She wants me to hurt the way she does.

My left hand comes free and I try to work at the right while Samantha and the Los Demons club member are distracted with each other. My right hand slips free and excitement pounds through my chest. Next, I wiggle my feet, trying to free my legs. I have one shot at doing this right. If I fuck up, I'm dead.

"Hurry up. Prez wants her finished and I have plans for you," he rasps out. Samantha sidles up close to him and whispers in his ear while running her nails through his dark hair. He grabs her ass and pulls her flush against him releasing a low growl. He kisses her bruised neck harshly and Samantha whimpers. I am not sitting through this while they maul each other. I'll throw up all over if I do. While they're busy practically fucking each other, I slowly reach my free hands in front of me and undo the ropes. This is why you use zip ties. They're harder to break out of.

Once my feet are free, I look to see what these two are doing. He has her pinned against the wall, her back to his front, grabbing her boobs and grinding into her from behind. Samantha's face is pushed against the wall, his free hand around her throat. She's mewling and begging for more. Neither of them are paying any attention to me. Thanking the Biker Gods for small miracles, I carefully pick up the metal chair I was tied to and carry it. I step behind the two and swing it as hard as I can, nailing the Los Demons in the back of the head. He releases an umph sound and falls into Samantha, pinning her to the ground.

"No, no, no. You can't do this!" She screeches struggling to get out from under his weight. I swing the chair again into the back of the Los Demon's head, making sure he doesn't get up. Blood seeps from his hairline and drips down onto the struggling woman under him. I toss the chair away and grab the ropes they used on me. I shove him off Samantha and put my knee into the center of her back. I yank her hair, making her immobile.

"I am doing this you stupid bitch. You don't think I don't see you, but I do. I see the vile heartless bitch you are." I tie her hands behind her back and lean down so I'm right next to her face. She tries to buck me off her, but I don't release my hold. "You think you're the only one Chains had harmed? You are far from right. He took something away from me. Something I will never get back. He took the choice away from me. You could've changed. You could've helped others, but you didn't. Now you'll pay for your mistakes." I stand up once I have Samantha secured and kick her hard in the stomach. Then I deliver a harsh blow to her face, knocking her out cold. I shove her into the corner of the small room away from the door and check the Los Demons pulse. There is none. I've killed him, I now have blood on my hands. I shove the thought in the back of my mind and search his cut for a weapon. My fingers land on a butterfly knife and I yank it free. I shove his dead body away and slowly creep toward the door.

I crack it open and peek outside. Two men guard the door with their backs to me taking up the whole hallway. How am I going to get out of this? I silently close the door and lean against it. Looking around the room, there is nothing in here but two bodies, one dead, one unconscious, the chair and a stand. That's it. No window to escape out of, no bed, no bathroom. It's stripped bare of everything else.

I inhale a deep breath knowing what I need to do. It's now or never. I flick the butterfly knife open and crack open the door again. The bass of the music muffles my footsteps allowing me to step behind the two men standing guard. I approach the smaller one on my right and slip my knife against his throat, making him bend down to my height.

"Drop the guns or I slice him from throat to dick and you watch his guts fall out," I demand. The guy I have immediately drops his weapon. The other man stares at me with death in his eyes. He has on the Enforcer patch for Los Demons. "Do it motherfucker." I press the knife against the first guy's throat and feel the blade sink into his skin. Blood trickles down his throat and a satisfied smile crosses my face.

"Think I'm joking? I've already killed one dickless fucker. I have no problem killing both of you." The bigger guy carefully sets his gun down and raises his hands. "Kick it toward me and get into that room. Don't say a fucking word or he's dead." The bigger guy kicks his gun in my direction and walks slowly toward the open door. He lunges for me at the last second and I hold strong. I press my knife against his buddy's throat and the blade sinks deep. He gurgles, fighting for air. I shove him into the bigger asshole, knocking them both into the room.

An explosion vibrates the whole club and I lose my balance falling to the dirty floor. Screaming and shouting from the other rooms echo down the hallway. Chaos ensues as more of Los Demons come flying past us toward the explosion. The Enforcer shoves his dead buddy off him and reaches for me. His hand grabs my ankle pulling me toward him. I kick and fight trying to loosen his hold on me. He squeezes hard, yanking me closer. My free foot connects with his face straight into his nose the cartilage crunching under my boot.

"Bitch!" he roars out blood dripping down his face. His grip doesn't falter and I shove the heel of my boot into his face again but miss as he dodges it at the last second. He yanks me toward him, trapping my legs under his big body. "You're going to fucking pay for that one little girl." The Los Demons Enforcer drags me into the room. I try to grab the door frame stopping him but he's so much stronger than me, my fingers lose their grip. He straddles my waist, his powerful body pinning me to the floor. Breathing heavily, the Enforcer shoves his long hair from his face and leans over me.

"I'm gonna have fun with you." His fingers wrap around my throat squeezing it slightly. "First, I'm gonna choke the fucking life out of you until you're begging for breath. Then when you think it's over, I'm gonna bring you back to life by fucking your lifeless body. Then after I'm through with that you'll beg me to kill you."

"Fuck you, asshole," I rasp out. He squeezes my throat until black spots don my vision and I can't breathe. I claw and fight with everything I have. Digging into the back of his hands trying to get him to release his brutal grip. I can't pass out. I won't pass out. My ears are ringing from lack of oxygen, my heart is pounding against my chest when dizziness takes hold.

Darkness invades my vision. I'm at the edge of death. I can't do it anymore. I can't fight him anymore. I relax my grip and fall limp into the void of death and life. Heavy footsteps pound toward me, but I'm done for. This is it; this is my last time here on earth.

Chapter 17

Blayze

We're on the rooftop waiting for our cue to enter the strip club. The night wind whips through my cut, deep into my bones. A strong feeling of dread clenches my stomach, gripping it until I can't breathe. Capone is watching me from his spot next to the door, his black eyes track my every movement.

Krimson and Nolan are hovered together next to the other side of the door in a heated conversation. I watch as Nolan moves a piece of Krimson's blonde hair from her face and cups it gently with his scarred hands. She holds his hands against her face and offers him a smile that lights up the night sky.

I'm envious of the two of them right now. I need my girl back so I can offer her the same comfort and she can light up my world again. Darkness and death are all I know right now until she's in my arms safe and sound.

A loud explosion echoes through the night, shaking the roof. That's our cue to go. I yank open the door and run down the stairs as fast as I can. I reach the bottom and crack open the metal door. Chaos unfolds before my eyes. All the Los Demons are running toward the front of the club. Girls are screaming and crying. Smoke billows into the front room. That's not my concern right now. My concern is getting into the back room and rescuing Monica. I turn right and head down the dark hallway. A Los Demon slams into me, not paying attention to where he's going. I quickly grab his head and twist his neck. He falls lifeless to the floor. I look around for more, but I can't see anyone in the darkness.

I find the door where Monica is being held. There are no guards out here, making my job easier. I reach for the doorknob when a sharp pain laces my right arm followed by a loud pop.

"Fuck, Blayze!" Capone shouts. Another loud pop rings through the darkness and the Los Demon who shot me falls to the ground dead. I look up at Capone and he has his gun out aimed at the now dead Los Demon. "You good?"

I move my arm and grit my teeth through the pain. "I'm fine. Thanks, brother." I turn the doorknob and shove the door open. Blinding red hot rage flows through my blood when I see a Los Demon hovering over Monica. His hands are wrapped around her throat, choking the life out of her.

I move quickly into the room and grab him by his cut throwing him against the wall. A gasp leaves the lips of someone behind me, but my focus is on this motherfucker right here putting his hands on my woman.

"You're a dead fucking asshole." I move quickly toward him and see he's their Enforcer. I deliver a painful blow to his already bloody face. He throws his hands up in defense, blocking my punches. I blank out and rain blow after deadly blow onto this cocksucker. He fucked with the wrong MC. The Royal Bastards take no mercy on anyone who harms what belongs to us.

My arms are weakening and the Enforcer isn't moving but that doesn't stop me. I stand above him sending kick after kick into his lifeless bloody body. Strong arms wrap around my shoulders yanking me back into the present. The pain in my arm comes at me full force and I scream out in pain.

I spin to attack the fucker who's holding me but it's Capone and he growls in my ear, "I've got you brother. It's me." He releases his brutal grip on my arms and lets me go. I turn around searching for Monica. My eyes land on her immobile body lying on the floor with Krimson hovering above her.

"No, no, no!" I cry hurrying over to Monica. I drop to my knees, hovering over her body, resting the palm of my hand against her flushed cheek, brushing away pieces of her dark hair. Her breathing is shallow and her heartbeat is weak. "Don't you dare leave me, Bug. Don't you dare." I scoop her limp body up into my arms and cradle her against my chest. Tears fall down my cheeks and I don't stop them. I don't give a flying rat's fucking ass if they see me cry. This is my life, my whole world. "Come back, Bug. Please, I can't do this without you."

Shouting, screaming and the loud pop of gunfire from the other section of the club grows quiet as everyone in here watches me.

"Blayze, we have to go," Capone rests his hand on my shoulder. I look into his eye and the blackness in them is hard and cold. He wants to murder a motherfucker for touching his sister. I know how he feels. I feel the same way, but right now Monica is my priority. I stand, holding her close to my chest. Her shallow breathing is hot against my skin. Thankfully, she's breathing on her own. But I still don't know how long she's been without oxygen and if there's any irreversible damage. Monica has been through so much already and has come out stronger on the other end, whatever is going on now, I'm confident she'll fight through it.

A low groan comes from the corner of the room and I stop walking toward the door, looking around. There are three dead bodies here and only one is mine. A smile graces my lips knowing my girl is responsible for the other two.

Another groan comes from the corner of the room and Krimson hurries over to it while Nolan and Capone watch the hallway. Krimson reaches down and yanks up a bruised and beaten Samantha, hog tied. Her face is bloody, her right eye is swollen shut and her head lobs from side to side.

"What do you want to do with her?" Krimson asks.

"Fucking kill her for all I care. The bitch is a traitor." I rumble glaring at the woman who's caused so much pain in just a little bit of time. Samantha's good eye grows wide with fear.

"Hold on a sec," Capone stops Krimson from snapping Samantha's neck. "She might have information as to why Chains had that photo on him."

"She doesn't," Monica chokes out coughing. I look down at my Bug with tears in my eyes. She's staring up at me, her brown eyes are full of love. "You can put me down. I'm OK."

Reluctantly I release Monica, sliding her down my body and she stands on her own two feet. I harden behind my jeans. I know this isn't the appropriate time, but Jesus fucking Christ this woman wakes the insatiable beast inside of me. She grips my arm tightly balancing herself until she has full strength, smirking at me. "What? I'm a guy, I can't help it."

Monica stands in front of me, pushing her plump ass against my hard-on and turns her attention to Capone.

I wrap my good arm around her shoulders holding her against me. "She doesn't know anything about Chains except he violated her the way he tried to with me." Monica's voice is weak but getting stronger with every word. "All this started because she was jealous of us. Her plan was to kill me and then become tight with all of you."

"You're a liar," Samantha growls.

Krimson grips Samantha's face tightening her fingers into her skin, "I suggest you shut the fuck up."

Samantha snaps her mouth shut and Monica continues, "She doesn't know shit. All she knows is that Los Demons wanted to hurt the Royal Bastards and she wanted the same thing. Samantha was dead the moment she started working with them against us. So, yeah kill the stupid cunt." Monica looks at me over her shoulder. "Take me home, Blayze."

Capone nods his head and Krimson wraps her slender fingers around Samantha's bruised neck. The crack sends a shiver down my spine. Krimson drops Samantha to the floor and steps over her dead body. Nolan reaches for her pulling Krimson against his hard body. He kisses the top of her head offering comfort.

Capone opens the door with his gun drawn and heads down the hallway. We meet Red, Tiny, Trigger, Bear and two of Nolan's men standing in the open bar area. Each brother has blood splattered on their cuts and jeans.

Bear spots us first and heads in our direction, "Thank fuck she's Ok." His big arms hug Monica's tiny body and a low growl escapes my throat. Chuckling Bear releases Monica and slaps me on my bad arm. I wince in pain but don't say anything. I can feel the warm blood drip down my arm and pool at my fingers.

"One problem, Prez." Trigger comes up to us with a menacing glare in his eyes.

"What?" Capone responds.

"Dread, Drew and two of their men got away. There must've been a secret exit we didn't know about. But we did find this in his office." He holds a notebook up and hands it to Capone. Capone flips it open reading it. His face doesn't show any emotion except the slight tick in his jaw and his black eyes narrow.

"What is it, Prez?" I ask through clenched teeth. I'm slightly dizzy from the blood loss but shake it off.

"He's not staying here. He's heading to Detroit. These are routes and channels they used to transport the missing girls from state to state." Capone reads more, lifts his eyes and stares at Krimson. "He's heading to Savage Saints, Detroit."

"Are you sure?" Krimson asks swallowing hard.

"Positive. Kayne will need back up out there if this gets too much out of his control." Capone flips the notebook closed and stuffs it in the inside of his cut.

The front door swings open and we all spin around with our guns drawn, pointing them at the door.

"Whoa. What a welcome," Torch jokes with his hands held high. Derange, Dagger and the last of Nolan's men come in through the door and head right for us. "We need to go, Prez. The cops are on their way."

Monica grabs my bloody hand and I grit my teeth. Her fingers slip through the blood and she pulls away staring at her soaked hand. "Blayze, you're hurt."

"I'm fine. Now let's move before we have to explain anything," I brush off Monica's worry and stride to the door. We don't have time for this shit.

"There's no way you're going anywhere right now," Monica glares at me. "Let me look and take care of it."

"It's fine. Just a flesh wound." I shrug my shoulder's gritting through the pain.

"I'll determine that. Now get your stubborn biker ass over here and let me look," the pleading in Monica's brown eyes does me in. I huff and stomp back to where she's standing.

"Fine," I concede. I remove my cut and drape it over my good arm. Monica lifts my black t-shirt peeling it away from my arm. I clamp my teeth and hiss through the pain.

"This is pretty bad, Blayze. We need to cover it and you're going to need stitches." Monica disappears behind the bar and my heart hammers against my chest when she's out of my sight. She pops her head back through the door and I breathe a sigh of relief. Jesus she's going to give me a heart attack.

Monica approaches me quickly with a bottle of Vodka and a clean towel. "This is going to hurt but will work for now." She tears the sleeve of my shirt off and pours the Vodka over the wound. My arm burns where she's dousing it in flames.

"Fucking shit woman. You about done?" I shout.

"Almost, you big baby," Monica gives me a small smile but the worry in her beautiful eyes is prominent. She takes the towel, rips it into several small pieces, wraps it around my arm and ties it off. "There, that should hold you over until we get back to the clubhouse and can get it stitched."

"Thanks, Bug. Now can we go?" I ask shrugging my cut back on.

"You're such a bastard, you know that right?" Monica pats my chest and gives me a small kiss.

"A Royal Bastard through and through." I tease resting my good arm across her shoulders.

All of us but Dagger walk out of the strip club and head to our bikes. He's staying behind to clean up the best he can before the cops show. Sirens are getting louder and louder in the distance. Once we reach our bikes, I hand Monica my helmet and help her strap it on. Once she's ready, I straddle the beast and wait for her to climb on. Monica settles behind me and wraps her arms around my waist, her body flush against my back, holding on tight. I push up the kickstand and fire up my Harley. Capone takes the lead and I'm right behind him with Trigger next to me. Followed by Torch, Red, Tiny, Bear, Derange and Krimson's crew behind us. My head is spinning but I push it aside and focus my attention on the road ahead of me so we don't end up with road rash.

It takes all my effort to ride back to the clubhouse but by all that is holy, I manage it. I feel the blood from my bullet wound seeping through the makeshift bandage. I pull into the garage behind Capone and drop the kickstand down. Monica dismounts and removes my helmet, waiting for me. I shut off my bike and climb off. Dizziness grabs at the edge of my body. Voices are echoing in the distance; I think they're shouting at me but they sound too far away to be sure. Pain laces my arm when I land on it and darkness takes hold.

Chapter 18

Capone

I turn just as my VP dismounts his bike. Watching his tanned face turn pale and he falls to the ground. Chaos ensues. Screams from my sister erupt on an ear-piercing level and I snap into action.

"Derange, get the fuck over here now!" I roar over the screaming. Kneeling next to Blayze, I take his hand in mine and his skin is cold to the touch. His breathing is shallow but steady. Bear wraps his arms around Monica trying to soothe her. Her screaming subsides to whimpers while her face is buried in his chest. She's mumbling something but I can't make out what she's saying.

Derange shoves his way through my brothers and kneels on the opposite side of Blayze. He checks his pulse and rips his shirt away from the bullet wound. Blood pours through the makeshift bandage Monica did up before we left.

"We need to get him into the surgery room. I have to stop the bleeding." Derange's pale blue eyes meet mine full of worry.

"Tiny and Torch, grab his feet. Red, help me with his head. Derange, keep pressure on the wound. We're going to move him." Everyone jumps into action. Tiny and

Torch lift Blayze's feet carefully while Red and I grab his shoulders. "Carefully lift him and move him into the surgery room. Fast but cautious." Derange is walking beside us, keeping his hand over the bullet wound. This motherfucker is heavier than he looks. Monica and Bear follow without another word.

We reach the room where my Tail Runner does his magic. Monica opens the door wide for us. Tears are leaking down her face, but she doesn't scream or cry. Our eyes meet for a brief second as I pass and her bottom lip trembles before she straightens her spine.

"Put him on the table," Derange orders. The surgery room is clean and sterile. Derange has everything he needs to doctor us up from stab wounds to gunshots to just being sick. I've asked him about it before and he used to study medicine back in the day before he patched in as a Royal Bastard. He doesn't go into his past a whole lot, but I know whatever it is, it was enough to send him packing and becoming a one-percenter.

Once Blayze is situated, I release his shoulders and stand off to the side. Derange shoves his blonde mop of hair out of his eyes and ties it back with a bloody hand. His head is shaved underneath right to the skin but he keeps the top long.

"I'll do my magic and let you all know how he's doing in a little while." That's our cue to leave.

Monica stands next to Blayze, gripping his limp hand tightly. "I'll stay and help. There's no way I'm leaving him."

"Fine but stay out of the way." Derange replies gruffly. He gets to work on stopping Blayze's blood flow and the rest of us file out of the room. Our heads are lowered and morale is low. Red approaches me with the rest of my guys behind him.

"What's the plan, Prez?"

"Right now? Nothing." I stare out into the common room. Not much activity going on out there. It's quiet enough to hear a pin drop. "Go and unwind. It's been a rough day."

My brothers all leave and head in their own direction. Some go directly to the bar and grab a drink; others go to the pool tables. No one goes very far waiting for word on Blayze. Someone turns up the music and the bass of Nagazi's newest hit pumps through the speakers.

Krimson and her crew left to head back to their place once we got Monica out of Bloody Scorpions strip club. She said she'd wait to see if we needed her again. I hope to fuck we don't.

I sneak off to see Danyella without her knowing I'm here. I watch from the shadows while she sits at the bar, nursing a drink one of the prospects poured for her. She stares off into space, oblivious to anyone and anything around her. Trigger saunters up next to her with all his biker swag and takes the empty stool. She doesn't even blink when he starts talking.

Rage pumps through my blood watching him. I clench my fists together, grinding my teeth. She's mine and no one will ever harm her again. I step from the shadows and pin Trigger with a glare so deadly he visibly shakes. He leans in and whispers something to Danyella and it takes all I have not to slit his throat. Trigger slides off the stool in pursuit of any other woman besides mine.

Danyella blinks rapidly and zeroes in on me. Her emerald eyes cut straight into my soul. My heart hammers against my chest and sweat beads on my brow. I've never felt this way before and from the tightness in my chest, I have no argument she means something to me. Danyella raises a perfectly manicured brow in my direction and ticks her head, motioning to the empty stool beside her.

I approach her with the confidence of the President of the Royal Bastards MC even though I'm nervous as hell. I wipe my sweaty palms on my jeans and motion to the prospect for a drink. He pours a finger of Jack into a glass and slides it in front of me. Twirling it around in my hand, I knock it back letting the alcohol burn down my throat and into my stomach.

"What's going on?" Danyella asks quietly. She leans her elbows on the bar and pushes away her drink.

"What do you mean?"

"I mean what's going on. Are we going to Michigan or not?" Her green eyes plead with me to tell her the truth. She deserves to know the truth but I don't know if she can handle it. She's been subjected to those asshole Scorpions and Los Demons for months. The more I look into both their clubs, the more reach they have than I thought.

I roll the empty glass in my hands and stare at the bar top. "Blayze has been shot and is now with Monica and Derange." I blurt out, ripping the Band-Aid off. Danyella sucks in a breath on a gasp. "He lost a lot of blood and passed out when we got back."

"What? Why didn't anyone come and get me?" The hurt in her voice is unavoidable. "I could be in there helping."

She rises from the stool, her drink long forgotten. I grab her thigh, stopping her from moving. Fire races up my arm from the contact and my erection stirs behind the zipper of my jeans. "Sit." One word from me and Danyella complies, which makes my dick turn to steel. She sinks back down onto the barstool. I don't remove my hand. I can't remove it. And she doesn't make me remove it either.

"I want to help my brother." The sadness in her eyes turns to lust in a second. Her long lashes flutter against her cheeks.

"I know you do, but he's in good hands. The best way to help is to wait here for Derange." My voice is soft and comforting, my fingers trace patterns on her thigh.

Danyella's gasp hitches in her throat. She drops her eyes to my hand and her cheeks turn red. Her chest heaves as her pink tongue darts out to wet her full red lips. I stifle in a groan. "Derek, what are you doing?" She whispers. Her eyes snap up to mine. Fear and nervousness replace the lust shining at me.

I yank my hand away quickly like I shoved it over a hot stove and blink. What the fuck am I doing? Danyella has had enough men manhandle her. She isn't ready for me yet. Tears form in her eyes as she watches me. "I'm sorry Derek. I'm so sorry."

"Don't ever apologize to me, Belle." The nickname I gave her years ago turns her face into a full-on blush. I take her small, slender fingers into mine and caress the backs of them in soothing motions. I stare into her shining green eyes that has a way of searing straight into my soul. "I didn't think about how you'd react. It was selfish of me to think we could pick up where we were heading when you disappeared." I inhale a deep breath and release it. "When you're ready, I'll be waiting." I peer into her eyes before dropping her hands and standing up. I have to get out of here before I do something we both will regret. I turn my back on Danyella and walk toward my room. I don't look back. I can't. If I see the pain in her soulful eyes, I will lose my shit. I'll resurrect every motherfucker who fucked with her and blast their fucking dicks off then blow their heads clean off their shoulders.

I reach the safety of my room and slam the door behind me with hard enough force the walls tremble. I lean against the door, sucking in a deep breath through my teeth and exhale it harshly. I need to keep my shit together. I can't expose my weakness. Someone already tried taking her away from me months ago just to hurt me and my club. I can't allow myself to give in to temptation and leave the door wide open for that again.

I pull out the picture that's been tucked away into my cut since I killed Chains. I unfold it and remove the creases. Vengeance burns through my bones as I stare at the photo.

A soft knock vibrates through the door and straight into my heart. It's Danyella. I can do the noble thing and ignore it. Or I can do the Bastard thing and let her in. I tuck the photo into the inside pocket of my cut and make a decision. I reach for the knob and twist.

Chapter 19

Blayze

"He's going to be fine. Too much blood loss but I've given him two transfusions. He should be coming around at any time." Derange speaks in a hushed voice to someone, but I can't open my eyes to see who.

Soft, warm hands wrap around mine and hold on with strength. I try to move but my body and brain don't want to cooperate. I lightly squeeze the hand holding mine and peek an eye open. My vision is blurry so I blink a couple of times, trying to focus.

"You're awake," Monica whispers against my ear sending a longing of want down my spine.

"Yeah, I am, Bug. Did you doubt me?" I whisper back. "Where am I?" I'm lying on a soft bed against a stark white wall. A sheet is settled over my waist. My shirt is off and a bandage wrapped around my bullet wound. Fire races down my arm when I try to move it and it itches like crazy.

Monica releases my hand and runs her fingers through my hair massaging my scalp. "Not in a million years." She smiles softly at me; her brown eyes are glistening with tears. "Listen, you lost a lot of blood but Derange was able to give you two blood transfusions. He has you in one of the extra rooms. How are you feeling now?"

"From a flesh wound? That's a little dramatic don't you think?"

"It wasn't a flesh wound, Xander." Monica levels me with an annoyed glare. "The bullet nicked an artery on the underside of your arm. You're lucky you didn't bleed to death."

"Blayze," Derange speaks from the other side of me. I turn my head to look at him and the pounding in my skull sends my stomach into a tight cramp. "It's going to take a few days for you to feel one hundred percent. I want you to take this time to rest and relax."

"I can't. There's too much going on for me to sit here." I try to sit up by my stomach has other ideas as I hold back a gag.

"You can and you will," Capone speaks from the doorway. "You look like shit, brother."

"Geez, thanks asshole," I grumble and lay back down.

"That's Royal Bastard asshole to you." Capone pushes off the door and enters the room. His black eyes are burning into me, daring me to go against his orders. Something's off with him, but I'm too tired to explore that right now. "You're going to rest and relax for the next couple of days."

"What about Dread, Drew and Los Demons? We can't let them get away." Just even the thought of those two escaping makes my blood boil.

"When you're healed, we're heading to Michigan. So, get the fuck better soon so we can get there." Capone heads out of the room but stops in the doorway turning back to me with worry in his dark eyes. "And Blayze. If you ever pull a stunt like that again, I will shoot you myself."

"Aye, Prez. I'll let you shoot me if it happens again." Capone grins and leaves the room.

Monica slaps my chest in annoyance. "You scared the hell out of me. Don't ever do that again."

I grab her hand and pull her down onto the bed with me, tucking her into my good side. "I'll try not to Bug, but I can't guarantee it. It's the way of our life. The code of honor we live by." My voice is getting groggy by the second but I don't want to waste any more time away from Monica.

"I know, Xander. I know the code. It's been ingrained in my brain since I was a child. But that doesn't mean I won't stop worrying about you." Monica's hand snakes down the sheet, resting on my abs while her warm breath fans across my neck sending a longing deep into my soul.

"And that's my cue to leave," Derange clears his throat.

"That'd be good right about now," I chuckle. "Unless you want to talk about what pops up next."

"Nope, sorry. That's not something I want to see. I'm gonna find me a woman to sink in to." Derange leaves the room, closing the door behind him.

"You're such a bastard," Monica mumbles into my chest.

"A Royal Bastard. Remember that." I cup the side of her face and bring her lips against mine. Licking the seam of her lips, Monica opens them with no hesitation. I enter her hot, wet mouth with any lack of care. It's been too long since I've had her wrapped around me, I can't wait any longer. A moan escapes Monica's throat and I swallow it up with a fevered kiss. "Mine," I growl against her lips.

"Yours, just like you're mine," Monica returns the frenzy kiss and straddles my waist, pushing the sheet down my legs. I love it when she gets all dominating on me. "Should we be doing this?" She pants against my lips.

"Bug, it's too late to stop now." I kiss down the silky column of her throat and a moan rips through her lips. "These need to come off." I slap Monica's ass with my good hand and she yelps.

She quickly removes her leggings and t-shirt, baring her sexy body to me, scars and all. I lick my lips, watching her fine ass as she turns and locks the door. Leaning against it, Monica pushes her chest out and sways her hips to a beat only her and I make.

"Fuck woman. I'm laid up in bed and you're teasing me. Get over here now," I growl through clenched teeth.

Monica saunters toward me, swaying her hips like a Goddess. "You want this big boy?" She teases.

"Fuck yes. Now bring that sexy body over here." I watch her eyes light up as she pushes my boxers down my legs and straddles me. She sinks down onto my swollen shaft and with all that is holy and unbelievable, Monica moves.

Together we make love like we've never done before. Our souls connect on a higher level as we both reach our peaks staring into each other's eyes. Lost in each other's possession.

I will die before I let another bad thing happen to my Bug. I will slaughter anyone who stands between me and her. I will burn the earth down in a blaze to get to her. I will sell my soul to the devil to make sure she is safe. Because I'm a Royal Bastard and that's what we do for the women we love.

We murder, we kill, we torture anyone who crosses us. I might not have had the full closure on what happened to my sister or to Monica, but I will. I will get my revenge on any asshole who fucks with me and my club.

*****

It's been days since I've been shot and I'm going stir crazy sitting here. Capone called a quick Church meeting at the asscrack of dawn and we're all piled into the sanctuary. Most of us are leaving for Michigan in a few hours, riding the whole way. It's just over two thousand miles across the country.

Capone slams the gavel onto the scarred oak table silencing the whole room. "In a few hours, we're leaving to visit the Savage Saints in Mt. Pleasant, Michigan. I talked to Jameson, at our Mother Chapter in New Orleans and he gave us the clear. I told them what was happening and he told me to handle it the Royal Bastards way." An evil smirk crosses Capone's face. One that instills fear in the biggest and baddest motherfuckers around.

Jameson is the President of our Mother Chapter in New Orleans and any type of move like this needs to be approved through him. We're going to be crossing into uncharted territories and need approval where to ride and with or without our colors.

"We will be passing through our other Chapters along the way and they agreed to let us stay on their compounds while we're traveling. We have the green light brothers." Capone raps his knuckles on the table. "So, those of you going with us need to pack your shit and be ready to roll by eleven. I want to get as far as I can today. Hopefully into our Nevada Chapter by sunset."

"I've mapped out the best route there," Tiny says pulling a United States map out and showing us the highlighted route. There is a bunch of X's and O's along with dash marks. I have no fucking clue what they mean but it's Tiny. He's the best at being our Road Captain so I'll go with what he tells us. "It's a six-hour ride to Tonopah, Nevada. If we leave at eleven, we can make it there by five. Rest for the night then head out to Idaho Springs, Colorado. It's a twelve-hour ride from Tonopah to Idaho Springs." He points to the map. Both Tonopah and Idaho Springs are marked with a red X. "We will stay the night at that Royal Bastards Chapter. It's another seven-and-a-half-hour ride to Lincoln, Nebraska and their Chapter. We can stop in and shoot the shit for a little while but then need to be back on the road. We will stop again in Ankeny, Iowa, which is three hours from Lincoln." Tiny points to the O on Lincoln and the red X on Ankeny. "There, we will stay the night again and head out in the morning. Ankeny will be our last stop on the way out there. Then we'll be in Mt. Pleasant at night fall by day four as long as everything goes good."

"What are the dashes on here?" I ask. This is the longest trip we've ever taken.

"The dashes are areas we need to avoid. Ones that are overrun with Bloody Scorpions and we won't have permission to enter." Tiny responds staring at the map. The Bastard is in his element. Usually, we do quick runs from here to San Francisco or San Diego. Sometimes into Mexico when the cartel wants their drugs run from us. Nothing to this extent.

"Everyone good to go?" Capone asks. No one answers him so he slams the gavel onto the table, ending our meeting. Quick and swift. The way our Prez does things.

Bear, Tiny, Red, Trigger and Torch stand to pack their shit. Tiny folds the map and puts it in the inside pocket of his cut. Derange and Dagger along with a few prospects are staying behind to guard our club. Monica is riding with me.

"What's my sister doing?" I ask Capone.

He turns his head and gives me a questioning look. "What do you mean?" Capone swallows hard and diverts his eyes like he's hiding something.

"My sister, Danyella. Is she making the trip with us or staying here?" Capone shrugs his shoulders but still won't look at me. That has the hair on the back of my neck stand on end. "Prez, what are you hiding?"

"Why in the fuck would I be hiding something?" He growls.

"Because you won't look at me," I state.

"Nothing. I haven't asked her if she wants to go. Why don't you find out?" He dismisses me with a nod of his head.

I push away from the table, "Fine. I will go and ask her. But I swear to fuck, if she refuses to go because of your bitch ass, we're going to have words."

"Blayze," Capone mumbles my name stopping me from walking out the door. "She came onto me the other night and I turned her away. She isn't ready for me yet and until she is, it's best if she keeps her distance." I glare at my Prez, my best friend. There's more to this story than what he's telling me, but he is my President and I'll respect. "One more thing."

I stare up at the ceiling praying to keep my shit together. I can't snap and disrespect my Prez. "What is it?"

"Drake from our Savannah Chapter paid us a visit when you were recovering. Some crazy shit is going on down there and he wanted to speak with Monica about the Black Railroad." Capone leans his elbows on the table.

"Did he talk to her?" My blood pressure is rising through the roof right now. Drake is one crazy motherfucker and I don't want him near my girl without me.

"No, he didn't get a chance to. His Ol' Lady had other plans and they left in a hurry. After he left, I dug a little more into it and the Black Railroad is how they're transporting the girls from state to state. I made a call to some other Chapters and it started in our Alaska Chapter."

"Why did he think Monica had something to do with it?"

"Because of that weasel dick James. Los Demons and Bloody Scorpions are balls deep in the Black Railroad. And James was running it through her studio. Right under our fucking noses and we had no idea."

"Well, he isn't going to be a problem anymore. Los Demons are eliminated. As for Bloody Scorpions, well, we're handling that shit."

"And we shut their channel down through this city. That's the plan, brother. Go get packed and see what Danyella is doing." Capone runs his hands through his dark hair. The stress of all this is weighing heavy on him.

"Aye, Prez. We're going to end this and quickly. Then we can get back to our lives." Capone offers me a curt nod and I leave Church, searching for my girl and sister.

Chapter 20

Blayze

We're about three hours into our trip towards Nevada. Danyella decided to go with us and she's currently riding on the back of Capone's bike. She refused to ride with him at first, choosing Torch but Capone wasn't having that. He practically growled and pissed and moaned until she gave in. She's keeping a safe distance from him but riding bitch on a bike is nearly impossible.

Monica on the other hand is pressed tight against my back, hanging on. Her hands keep drifting down and it's making riding hard, literally. I love the way she's pressed against me, the way she's wrapped around me.

We stop for gas and a break when we get close to Tonopah, Nevada. The summer sun is moving to the west and once it drops, the temps out here will drop dramatically too. The dry air surrounds me, making me sweat in my cut and jeans. Everyone is hot, pissy and miserable. Monica is talking to Danyella and from her body language, Monica is close to losing her patience. Danyella's eyes keep wandering toward Capone who's pacing back and forth talking on his phone.

Capone snaps his phone shut and heads in our direction. "We're all set to stay at Crossroads. Grim is setting us up with rooms. Monica and Danyella, you stay with us and don't wander off on your own unless you're wearing a property of or Ol' Lady cut."

"Really, Capone? I'm not property or anyone's old lady." Danyella grumbles and crosses her arms over her chest.

Capone glares at her, his jaw ticking like a time bomb. "You are on this trip," he growls.

I let them argue it out, reach into my saddlebag and pull out a cut, "Bug," I say with a low tone. Monica turns her brown eyes toward me. Her whole face lights up with a huge smile when she sees what I have in my hands. "Will you wear my colors?" I open the cut and show her the patches sewn on. Over the right breast is her name and the left is Ol' Lady and below it is Property of Blayze. On the back is our Royal Bastards rockers.

"I'd love too Blayze." Monica shrugs off her riding cut I bought for her years ago and takes the new one in her small hands. She puts it on with gentle care and pops her hip out, posing. "Well? What do you think?"

"I think I'm gonna fuck you wearing just this later." I yank her closer to me and kiss her deeply. Monica complies and wraps her arms around my neck. Catcalls and whistles erupt behind us and I break our kiss grinning. "Dirty motherfuckers," I rumble against Monica's lips. She giggles and kisses me again.

"Let's roll before the sun goes down," Capone barks. He's still pissed at Danyella but that's something they have to figure out on their own. She's now wearing a property of Capone cut and isn't happy about it at all.

"I'll talk to her later and try to figure out what's going on inside her head," Monica promises me.

"I'd appreciate that. Hop on my sexy Bug. The sooner we get there, the faster I can get inside you." I swat Monica's ass and straddle my bike. She climbs behind me and wraps herself around my back.

We take off in formation down the Nevada highway. About an hour later we pull into a paved driveway and park our bikes alongside several others. We made it to our Tonopah Chapter. Two guys are standing outside and head in our direction when we stop. They both give off a different vibe I can't quite place.

"Capone, great you could make it," Grim, the President of the Tonopah Chapter stretches out his hand and Capone grabs it, giving him a brotherly slap on the back. "This is my Enforcer Azrael." He motions to a scary motherfucker with day of the dead makeup on.

"Thanks for having us brother. We appreciate the hospitality." Capone answers. He does the same with Azrael.

I dismount my bike after Monica climbs off and we walk together toward the two. My arm protectively draped around her shoulders.

"Azrael? Isn't that the name for Angel of death?" Danyella pipes up intrigued.

Azrael turns his attention in her direction and spots the property patch. "You're very knowledgeable, little one. Better keep that pretty mind on hold while you're here or things could get ugly quick."

Danyella shrinks back behind Capone and doesn't say another word. Tension is thick in the air when Capone speaks. "This is my VP, Blayze and his Ol' Lady, Monica." He points to me and Monica. Grim offers me his hand and I accept giving him a brother slap on the back. Azrael does the same. Introductions are made with each member and Grim shows us inside.

Once we're settled in our rooms, Monica with me and Danyella with Capone, I release an exhausted sigh, flopping down on the soft bed.

"How's your arm?" Monica settles next to me and runs her fingers over my cut.

"A little achy but nothing I can't handle." I turn my head in her direction and stare into her beautiful brown eyes.

"That guy scares the shit out of me," Monica blurts out then slaps her hand over her mouth.

"Which one?"

"Azrael. He's got this creepy don't fuck with me vibe that's a little unsettling. I'll bet he's a great guy and protects his loved ones, but that makeup gives me the shivers." Monica shudders cuddling up against my side.

"They all have it, but they're our brothers. No matter what kind of vibe you're getting, don't say a word. Respect the patch and our brothers."

"I will. Don't worry about it. It's probably because I'm not used to them."

A hard knock on my door draws our attention to it. I lift my tired body off the bed and open it. Capone is standing on the other side.

"Grim just got word that a couple of Bloody Scorpions are at a bar close by. Let's go." He turns on his heels and leaves. My fingers curl into the door frame, my knuckles turning white. This might be what we're looking for.

I release my grip from the door and stalk toward Monica. "I have to go." I kiss her hard and quick before pulling away. "Stay here or in Capone's room with Danyella."

"Aye, aye, VP. Stay safe." Monica smiles.

I turn and leave finding Capone, Grim and Azrael on their bikes waiting for me. I signal with my head I'm ready and we all take off toward the bar.

Pulling into the stone driveway, the Nevada night nips at my nose. Grim and Azrael park next to us and pull their skull masks down.

"Message from Bodie's Ol' Lady was two Scorpions came in here and were sitting in the back. That was a half-hour ago." Grim reports climbing off his bike. Azrael, Capone and I climb off our bikes.

"Then let's go check it out." Capone gruffly responds. We all head inside and look around the dimly lit bar. Only a few customers are scattered around. It's deathly quiet the moment we walk in and all eyes turn in our direction. A girl tending bar motions with her head and Grim stalks toward her.

"They left about fifteen minutes ago. I tried to keep them here but something spooked them and they left." She tells us, putting four beers on the counter. "On the house. They were sitting in the corner booth." She points to the booth they were just at.

"Might as well drink one before we head back," Grim grabs his beer and heads toward the spot. Once we're all settled in, beer in hand, Grim asks the question I've been hoping to avoid. "What have they done to you?"

Capone takes a long pull before answering. "They kidnapped Blayze's little sister and was using my sister's, who happens to be Blayze's Ol' Lady's, porn studio as a drop off point for the Black Railroad. They were running women through it right under our noses. The man my sister was working with was involved. That's how they kept it from us. Until we finally caught her partner raping one of them in her studio. It all unraveled from there."

I grip my beer bottle tightly in my hand, surprised it doesn't shatter. "They took my girl, but we got her back before they could do irreparable harm. They've been dealt with but three got away. No one fucks with my girl or my sister." My voice is deep and rage is building up inside of me thinking about what has happened.

"Did you find your sister?" Grim asks intrigued by our story.

"Yes. She came with us. The little girl asking questions about Azrael." Capone pins Azrael with a glare. It's not out of spite or disrespect. "She's off-limits to everyone."

Azrael nods his head and grins. It looks sinister with all his makeup on. "You care about her."

"I do," Capone confirms. "She's mine when she's ready, only she hasn't figured it out yet."

Grim and Azrael grunt in response and we finish our beer, talking about club life and what's next. We have a long ride ahead of us tomorrow, so we leave the bar and ride back to Crossroads.

Once I find Monica with Danyella in Capone's room, we head back to ours. Arms and legs intertwined. I wanted to properly fuck my girl but my head and body weren't on the same page. Exhaustion took over and we both fell asleep.

Chapter 21

Blayze

Riding into the summer sun, I'm at peace even if it's short-lived. We're on the last day of our trip and should arrive in Mt. Pleasant by nightfall. We stopped at our sister Chapters on the way and a few times we had to help deal with some club shit.

Monica and Danyella got to meet some other members' Ol' ladies and they exchanged numbers to keep in contact. Danyella has been warming up to Capone some more. Whatever grudge she was holding when we left is slowly disappearing. Either that, or he was finally able to reason with her and made her realize she needs to figure herself out before they move forward.

The Welcome to Indiana sign is a sight for sore eyes. One more state to go then we're there. Capone signals to pull off at the next rest area and we follow. This ride has been long and treacherous for us. I can't wait till it's over and things get back to normal.

Capone sets his kickstand down, climbs off his Harley and stretches. He motions for me to come over and I do, leaving Monica behind.

"Kayne sent me a text. Said shit's all set up for us when we get there. Wanted to forewarn us Steam is off his rocker and shit's going to get real, fast. We won't have time to settle before we head for Detroit. We'll get a good night's sleep and head out first light."

"Aye, Prez. Does he know what's happening?"

"Yeah, he does. Said there's someone we need to meet when we get there. Pretty cryptic though." Capone runs his fingers through his dark hair and squeezes the back of his neck. Cars and pickup trucks drive past us, pulling into other parking spots. "I'm having a bad feeling about this, brother."

"It's almost over, Prez. Once we get the Bloody Scorpions taken care of and I get my revenge on Steam, we can go back to our lives. Go back to the coast and forget this ever happened." I rest my hand on Capone's shoulder, gripping it tight.

"Forgetting will never happen but we can move forward from this point on," Capone releases a deep breath and looks at Danyella. There's a longing in his black eyes. He's always had a soft spot for my sister and I can't blame him. I've been in the same situation with Monica. So close, yet so far away until recently. "It'll come when it's time. You have to believe that."

"I do." Capone nods his head. Bear, Tiny, Red, Trigger and Torch all make their way over to us, leaving the girls alone.

"What's the plan, Prez?" Bear asks cracking his neck from side to side.

"We'll be at the Savage Saints clubhouse in about six hours. Kayne has set up our rooms. We'll get there, get some much-needed rest and ride to Detroit tomorrow morning. Give Steam a surprise visit. Hopefully, if everything goes the way we want, Drew and Dred will be there like we think and it'll be over."

Tiny cracks his large knuckles. Trigger runs his hands through his shaggy hair and Red crosses his arms over his leather vest.

"Then let's roll. The longer we stand here, the later it'll be. I don't know about the rest of you, but some beer and bunnies sounds great after this long ride." Bear grunts.

"You heard the man. Beer and bunnies coming up," Capone cracks a smile and we all mount our bikes. Monica climbs on behind me, looking hot as fuck in her Ol' Lady cut. Once all this is over, I've decided I want to make it official. Once we get back to our clubhouse, I will ask her to marry me. Turn her from not only my Ol' Lady but my wife. I'm going to put a ring on her finger.

"You ready?" Monica's sweet breath fans in my ear when she leans into me, driving me wild with need.

"Fuck yeah, I'm ready to get you alone and give you a proper fucking," I turn my handlebars, raise my kickstand and hold the weight of my bike with my thighs.

Monica snakes her hands around my waist, "Promises, promises." She grabs my junk through my jeans, squeezing.

"Oh, it's definitely a promise I'm keeping, Bug. All the teasing you do all day for the last three days, I'm going to fuck you hard the moment we get to Savage Saints." I fire up my bike drowning out her response. She let's go of my dick after another squeeze and rests her head on my shoulder blades.

Capone pulls out of the rest area with Danyella holding onto him and I follow. Tiny, Red, Trigger and Bear follow behind me. Almost there, almost to the end.

Several hours and a few stops later, we pull onto a long driveway in the middle of nowhere. One thing I noticed about Michigan is the flatlands surrounding us. My body is fighting the time zone change and even though it's around dinner time, my body wants to think it's earlier than that.

A big white house comes into view after we come around a bend, idling our bikes. A porch full of bikers greet us wearing Savage Saints cuts as we park next to some other Harleys. The guy I went off on back in L.A., Blayde, comes off the porch heading right for me. His long stride eats up the space between us quickly. Monica stiffens behind me and I give her leg a gentle pat. Kayne, Savage Saints Prez, brushes his blonde hair out of his face and goes to Capone. They exchange greetings, giving each other a pat on the back. Blayde stares at me, his blue eyes questioning.

"Good to see you brother," Blayde extends his hand for me to shake. "No hard feelings from what went down in L.A." I grip his hand and shake it. His peace offering means our staying here could be a good thing. His eyes roam over Monica and my protectiveness rears its head. "Monica, those colors look better on you than mine did. Do over?"

I can feel her squirming behind me. She's uncomfortable, but she's got to face what happened head on. "Do over. Thanks, Blayde." She reaches out her hand and Blayde accepts it. Siren comes up behind Blayde and rests her hand on his arm. Her long dark hair flows down past her waist and a genuine smile graces her lips. Monica releases Blayde's hand and he drapes it over Siren's shoulders, giving her a kiss on the head.

"Welcome, I'm sure you guys are ready for some fun and relaxation after this long trip. Poison, Holly and I prepared a big dinner for you and a big party will be underway in a few hours. Come in when you're ready." Siren gives Blayde a kiss and heads back in the house.

"She's nice," Monica says, climbing off the back of my bike.

"With everything she's been through, still keeping a smile on her face is remarkable," Blayde replies watching Siren's ass sway as she walks away. "If you'll excuse me, I have some business to take care of."

Blayde leaves us standing there and follows Siren inside. Monica bursts out laughing drawing the attention of the rest of Savage Saints and Royal Bastards. Capone cocks an eyebrow at his sister's outburst and I shrug my shoulders. Kayne smirks and Stryker's eyebrows are scrunched together in confusion. I shake my head and pull Monica close to my side. She holds in her giggles.

"Everything OK, Bug?" I ask.

"It's perfect, Blayze." Monica sighs, turning her body toward me and gives me a small kiss on the lips. "I think we got the closure we both needed. I'm happy he's happy and there are no feelings what-so-ever. Siren is just what he needs." Monica grips my cut with both hands and stares up at me. The look that passes in her eyes is full of lust and want. "Now it's your turn to give me what I need."

"Where's our room?" I shout. Laughter rings out around us.

"Follow me and I'll show you," Kayne heads toward the house. I grab our bags out of my saddlebags and follow him inside with Monica tucked under my arm. Kayne walks up a set of stairs and opens the first door we come to. "You two can use this room."

We walk inside and I set our bags down on the king size bed in the room. "Thanks for this Kayne. We're going to freshen up and be down in a little while."

"I'm grateful you're here. Steam needs to be stopped at all costs." Kayne extends his hand and I accept, giving him a bro hug. "Take your time. Dinner will be ready in about an hour."

Once Kayne shuts the door behind him, Monica is on me. I crash my lips onto hers, swallowing the moans escaping her throat. I grip her ass pulling her against me. I yank her cut off and gently lay it on the bed. I remove my cut, laying it next to hers. Next is my T-shirt, jeans and boots. Monica strips down to her bra and panties. My mouth waters dying to taste every inch of her skin.

"Lay on the bed," I growl low.

Monica's eyes light up and she scurries to the bed. I crawl my way up her body, kissing each part of her skin along the way. We make love for as long as we both can. Spent, I lean in, kissing Monica softly pushing her sweaty hair from her forehead.

"I love you, Monica."

"I love you, too, Blayze."

I lay on the bed beside her, totally spent and ready to sleep when there's a knock on the door. Grumbling, I sit up and pull my boxers on. Monica grabs my T-shirt and goes into the bathroom, giving me and whoever's on the other side some privacy. I yank on my jeans, leaving them unzipped and throw open the door. Capone, Kayne and Blayde are standing on the other side. Capone has his fist raised like he's going to knock again.

"Good, you're not busy," Capone smirks before entering my room. I open the door wider to let the other two in and motion with my hand.

"Not anymore," I grumble. "What's up?" I sit on the bed waiting.

"Where's Monica?" Capone asks.

I point to the bathroom and the shower kicks on. "Freshening up. What's going on? I'd like to join her."

Capone speaks first, "Steam has no idea we're here or why."

"Yeah, I kind of figured that." I raise an eyebrow and cross my arms over my shirtless chest.

"Kayne has someone we need to meet. So, get dressed and meet us in the garage out back. I'm going to find Danyella and let her know we'll be a little bit." Capone mutters and I smirk.

"She has your balls already and you're not even fucking."

"Shut the fuck up, V.P. That's your sister." Capone barks.

"And I just thoroughly fucked yours so what's the difference?" Capone growls at my remark. "We're all adults here. Consenting adults. I'm sure these two don't want the details into my sex life or yours either so let's argue about it later. I'll let Monica know what I'm doing and be down in a minute or two." Capone huffs and heads for the door. "Hey Capone?"

He stops at the door and looks at me from over his shoulder. "What?"

I turn my head to make sure Monica isn't standing in the room. "When we get home, I'm going to ask the little vixen to marry me. With your permission of course."

"It's about time, V.P." Capone walks back toward me and slaps me on the back. "I'd be a fool to let her marry any other idiot." A smile graces his lips. "Of course, you have my permission. Now go let her know what you're doing and we'll meet you down there."

"Thanks, brother." I shake his hand and give him a bro hug, slapping his back. Kayne and Blayze congratulate me and they all leave the room. No rest for the wicked.

Thirty minutes later, I come down the stairs, fully satisfied yet again, and follow the smell of ham into the kitchen. A short girl with long curly brown hair is standing at the window staring out into the back yard. She doesn't hear my heavy boots approach her and she jumps.

"Holy hell. You scared the crap out of me," she places her small hand over her chest. "I'm Holly, Stryker's Ol' Lady,"

"Blayze, nice to meet you, Holly." I extend my hand and she grips it, giving me a strong shake. "What are you watching for?"

"Nothing. Just getting inside my own head." Holly's face turns red from embarrassment as she pulls her hand away quickly.

"I understand that." Awkwardness stifles the air around us. "Well, I'm going to look for Kayne." Holly doesn't acknowledge me; she just stares back out the window lost in her own head again already. I open the back door and let it close behind me, breathing in the warm country air. Back at our place the air is a salty dryness. This is clean and refreshing.

I meet Capone on the porch and together we walk down the stairs and head toward the garage out back. Heavy metal music is thumping the closer we get. The side door is opened a crack and I peek my head inside. My eyes adjust to the darkness and my blood runs cold. In the center of the room are two men wearing Bloody Scorpions cuts. Their arms are suspended above their heads wrapped in chains dangling from the ceiling. Their bare feet don't quite reach the ground. I step inside the garage, an inferno blazing through my body. I feel Capone stiffen next to me, rage radiating off his body.

"How in the fuck did you get this piece of shit here?" My eyes burn into the first man strung up. The man who has wreaked havoc on my sister. Dred, the President of Bloody Scorpions, stares at me through swollen eyes. His partner, Drew isn't moving or breathing.

"You know this piece of shit?" Stryker asks stepping next to me.

"Yeah, I know this motherfucker." I clench and unclench my fists at my sides.

"Wait a minute!" Capone barks. "I thought these assholes were in Detroit with Steam."

"They were," Kayne responds. "Steam had other ideas for this cuntwaffle. Looks like we don't have to go to Detroit for answers. They're right here. Rooster found both of them on the surveillance videos this morning. We grabbed them before you guys got here and had a little fun. What'd he do?"

"He's the one who kidnapped and raped my sister." I spit out through clenched teeth. "He's responsible for the disappearances of all the women we saved. Some of their deaths too."

"Is that right?" Kayne steps in Dred's face, slapping it with a metal cane he has in his hands. "Is that true? You're a rapist and kidnapper?"

"Fuck you, I don't answer to you," Dred mumbles through his swollen jaw.

"Oh, you'll answer me alright. Once I'm finished with you, you'll be begging me to end your life." Kayne pulls his arm back and swings with everything he has landing a solid blow to Dred's ribs. He swings back and forth and sucks in a breath but doesn't say anything.

Kayne raises his weapon again and hits Dred in the knee. I can hear the shatter of bones from my spot. Dred screams in pain.

"Well? Are you ready to answer some questions motherfucker?"

"Fuck you." Dred spits blood on the floor near Kayne's feet.

"I think it's time to let the girls play." A seductive voice responds from behind me. I spin around and see Poison and Siren enter the garage. Poison has on a Savage Saints cut with Cleaner over the breast and Ol' Lady below it. They have murder in their eyes. Behind them are Monica and Danyella.

"What the fuck is this a fucking sleepover?" Stryker growls when all the girls walk in.

"No, you brooding asshole. We're here for justice. You can't let this motherfucker get away with what he did to her." Poison points to Danyella whose eyes are wide with fright staring at Dred and Drew.

"Watch your tone, Poison." Stryker's nostrils flare.

"I'm a part of this MC just as much as you are. So, when you're an asshole, I will tell you. I won't ever disrespect our Prez, but you and I are going to have issues if you don't rein it in. You will respect me just as much as I respect you." Poison argues crossing her arms over her chest.

I am watching them both, waiting for someone to do something. Stryker laughs and brings Poison in for a hug. What the fuck? Capone and I exchange a glance and I shrug my shoulders. Not my club, not my business.

"Ok, that's enough," Kayne growls. Stryker releases Poison and she saunters to Kayne swaying her hips. "Poison, what makes you think she needs retribution like you two did?"

"Look at her, Prez. She's a fucking mess. She doesn't sleep, doesn't eat and won't talk to anyone. She's screaming for help and no one is listening." A lonely tear falls down Poison's cheek and she quickly wipes it away. "Fucking hormones."

"You ready to tell me what the fuck is going on with you?" Kayne asks, his voice is full of concern.

"Not now," Poison gives him a kiss.

"Is this true, Danyella? Is this why you're hot and cold with me?" Capone asks slowly approaching her. She's trembling from head to toe, nodding her head with tears streaming down her face. "Oh, fuck. I'm such an idiot." Danyella sobs collapsing onto the garage floor and Capone gathers her into his arms, soothing her.

Monica comes next to me and rests her head on my chest. I wrap her in my arms, breathing a little easier.

"She needs this, Blayze. More than anyone could know." Monica looks up at me and I wipe the tears away gathering in her eyes. "Trust me."

"Like you needed it?" She nods her head. "Ok, Bug. If you say so." I give her a small kiss. "Prez," Capone looks at me with rage in his eyes. "Let her have at him."

He whispers something to her and she shakes her head. He whispers again and together they stand. He grabs her hand and they walk toward Dred. Capone kicks him once in his bad knee causing Dred to howl in pain.

"Wake up motherfucker. I have a surprise for you." He punches him in the stomach causing him to swing back and forth. Dred peels one eye open and it settles on Danyella. He hisses through his broken jaw.

"I'll fuck you up again little bitch."

I watch Danyella transform from weak and timid to a strong and powerful woman. No longer afraid of the man in front of her, she stiffens her shoulders and swings with all her power landing a solid blow to his face. Dred screams out in pain as Danyella punches him repeatedly. Each blow hitting him hard.

"You piece of shit asshole." She brings her fist back and nails him in the nuts. "That's for touching all those girls." Dred howls. Danyella grabs his dick with her palm and squeezes hard. His face turns a deep shade of red and he grinds his teeth. "That's for forcing yourself on them."

Danyella squeezes his balls harder. I can hear the pop of one from my spot and I cover my junk. She pulls back making his body follow her. He's bucking his hips trying to get out of her grasp but he's at her mercy.

"This is for me. Each time you stuck your filthy dick down my throat or inside of me when I didn't want it. It's for each time you made me cry or made me bleed. Welcome to hell motherfucker. I'm your judge, jury and executioner." She balls up her other hand into a fist and keeps ahold of Dred's balls with the other. Danyella lets her fist fly, punching him square in the stomach. Dred's body swings back from the blow but she hangs on to his junk and I can hear the pop of the other one. My stomach clenches at the thought while Dred screams in pain. Blood blooms on his jeans and Danyella releases him. "Now tell these boys what they want to know, or I'll rip off your dick, shove it down your throat and let you choke."

I step up next to Danyella and put my arm around her shoulders, pulling my sister into my embrace. "Well done sis. Now let us take over." She nods her head, breathing heavily. Dred is close to passing out but we don't want him to yet. Danyella goes to Monica out of my line of sight. I turn my attention to Dred. "Why are you here?"

"Steam made us come here to kill you." Dred coughs up blood and spits it out at my feet.

"Looks like you fucked up. Say goodnight motherfucker." I bring my fist back and land a crushing blow to Dred's throat. He gasps for air but can't get any in. I crushed his windpipe. He flops around like a fish trying to breathe out of water before he stops moving. His lifeless eyes stare at me and I smirk. "That's what happens when you fuck with the Royal Bastards."

"Is it over?" Danyella asks behind me.

"Yeah, it's over. He'll never touch you or anyone else again." I respond.

"Thank God. What about Aerial and the rest of the girls?" Danyella is always putting others over her and it's a rare trait to find anymore.

"We'll find their homes and help them any way we can." Capone offers. Danyella nods her head.

"Can you please get me out of here?" She begs Capone.

He locks his arms around her and gives her a gentle kiss on the head. "You got it." Together they leave the garage. I watch from afar hoping and praying that she'll find her way out of this mess.

"Get the prospects to clean up the bodies." Kayne orders Stryker.

"You got it, Prez." Stryker walks out of the garage leaving me, Monica, Kayne, Poison, Siren and Blayde alone.

"Come on Monica, let's go see if Holly needs any help for dinner." Poison and Siren both put their arms around Monica. "Then you can give us the deets on that hunky man you snagged," Kayne growls but Poison winks at him. "You're still my hunky man." This seems to work because Kayne stops growling.

"Remember Princess, I'm the only one who can fuck you into oblivion." Poison's face turns red and Kayne smirks. "Be ready for me. I'll be in in a few." She nods her head and the three of them leave.

"Listen, I'm really sorry for you guys coming all this way for this short of a time." Kayne apologizes.

"Don't worry, brother. It was something that had to be done and I'm glad it was resolved so quickly. It makes me wonder what Steam is up to though." I think aloud.

"I've been wondering the same thing. But he's off his rocker. Has been for a long time. That's a problem Savage Saints can handle."

"We're here for a few more days so if you need help, just say so. Ride or die, brother." I offer my fist and Kayne bumps it.

"Ride or die. Now let's get some grub and party like no tomorrow."

Epilogue

Blayze

It's been a few months since we've been back from our trip. We stayed in Michigan for a few days longer than planned. Jameson, our Mother Chapter President, called Capone, so he had to head to New Orleans then Baltimore and meet up with the Presidents from other Chapters. He didn't say much when he got back but from the haunted look in his black eyes, it wasn't good.

Now, we're back at our clubhouse in Cali. The vibe here is peaceful and relaxing for the first time in a long time. We've been able to place most of the missing women back with their families, but some of them stayed instead of going home. Daisy is one of the few who stayed. She's recovering remarkably well from her gunshot wound. We still can't locate Aerial's mom, but Red isn't giving up. Danyella has been staying at our house more often with them than here at the clubhouse, but it's her choice. She's trying to find herself and what she wants to do with her life.

My brothers and I are standing in the common room where the pool tables used to be. The club bunnies and girls have transformed this part of the clubhouse into something beautiful. There are small white chairs set up in aisles that currently hold the bunnies, prospects and the rest of the Royal Bastards. Flowers are placed every fucking where and the spot I'm standing at is on a white throw rug. Dagger is standing on a podium behind me dressed in his leathers. Capone is right next to me on my left. I nervously adjust my cut waiting for Monica to get her ass out here. I wipe my sweaty palms on my black jeans. Capone cocks an eyebrow at me. Torch smirks and Bear, Derange, Red, Trigger and Tiny are squeamish. They keep wiping the sweat from their brows or fidgeting. They're the ones who shouldn't be nervous.

"Are you sure about this?" Trigger asks, adjusting his jeans for the hundredth time. He's the worst one out of all these guys with nerves.

"Of course, I am. I've never been surer about anything in my life." I answer honestly.

Capone dangles a set of keys in my face and smirks. "Do you like the Harley I picked up the other day? You know, the brand-new, satin black Sport Glide with the Milwaukee-Eight one-oh-seven-engine and high-performance suspension?"

"Yeah? That bitch is beautiful." I'm confused about where Capone is going with this.

"What if I tell you that if you don't go through with this, that bitch is yours?"

Realization dawns on me and I laugh. I laugh so hard my stomach hurts. "You're such a fucking asshole," I grumble once I have myself under control. "No way in hell. My girl is more important than that."

Capone pockets the keys and smiles huge. "That's Royal Bastard asshole to you, fuckface. Perfect answer. Welcome to the family officially, Blayze." Capone holds his hand out for me to shake. I grab his offered hand and he pulls me in for a hug. "Keep her happy. That's all I ask."

"I plan on it, brother." We release each other and turn toward the bar. Aerial comes flying down the hallway wearing a white lace dress and gray DC shoes. When she sees us standing here, she slows down and smiles.

"They're ready!" she shouts. Aerial has become the little sister of the Royal Bastards. We try to shield her from the parties the best we can, but she always ends up sneaking around and seeing more than she should. She's a sassy, sneaky little girl that keeps us on our toes but also brings a ray of sunshine to the brothers. She's quickly worked her way into our hearts and we will do anything to protect her.

Aerial plays with the lace of her dress, waiting until Daisy and Jezebelle make their way next to the bar, followed by Danyella. They're each wearing slim-fitting satin blue dresses; they did their makeup to perfection and their hair is in some fancy up do. I can't see the woman I've been waiting my entire life for yet and I'm nervous as hell. I keep shifting from foot to foot, anxious to lay my eyes on the perfect woman made just for me.

Soft music floats around us as Aerial makes her way down the makeshift aisle. She's counting her steps as she goes. Sometimes, she'll speed up and then make herself slow down. Once she reaches us, she turns and stands at the opposite end of where we are with a big smile on her tiny face. Jezebelle is next, her eyes never leave Derange's as she makes her way toward us. Once she reaches the end, she stands next to Aerial. Behind her Daisy walks down the aisle, followed by Danyella. Danyella keeps sneaking glances at Capone but his face is static, not releasing his scowl.

The music changes and everyone stands up. I can't see past the sea of heads until Monica steps up at the end of the aisle. She's the most stunning woman I've ever laid eyes on. In a long white dress that hugs her body like a second skin, Monica's eyes meet mine. She walks toward me with confident steps. Her brown eyes sparkle with love, a smile on her face that lights up the whole room. I adjust my growing erection in my jeans and a look of lust flashes in Monica's eyes. She finally reaches me and I grab her offered hand pulling her flush against my body.

"You look incredible, Bug." I nuzzle the curve of Monica's neck and nip at the skin with my teeth. She giggles and a soft moan floats between us.

Dagger clears his throat behind us, "Save that for after." The room erupts in whistles and catcalls. I reluctantly release Monica and turn us towards Dagger.

He raises his hands and the room quiets down. "Please be seated." Once everyone behind us sits, he begins. "We're gathered here today to witness the holy union of Monica Gates and Xander Blayze Combs. These two have been through many trials and tribulations in their lives and always manage to make it back to one another, no matter how much or how long they're separated. If anyone here believes these two should not be married, speak now or forever hold their peace."

The room grows silent when Dagger asks the question. I hold my breath, waiting for someone to make a smartass remark. But none come and I exhale loudly. "Thank fuck." The room erupts with laughter and Dagger quiets them down again.

"Very well. Do you Xander take Monica as your lawfully wedded wife?"

"You bet her sweet ass I do. She's mine." I stare into Monica's eyes when I answer. She's smiling at me so big; it lights up the entire room.

"Monica, do you take Xander to be your lawfully wedded husband?"

"I do, without a doubt," Monica says.

"The rings?" Dagger asks, holding his hand out for them. Capone reaches into his cut and produces two gold bands and places them in Dagger's palm. I had them custom made with our Royal Bastards logo etched into each band. On her band it reads, Property of Blayze. On mine, it has Property of Bug. He hands one to me, "Repeat after me. I, Xander Combs, take you Monica Gates as my wife. To have and to hold, in sickness and health. With the wellbeing of the Royal Bastards in mind, I will always put you first."

I repeat what Dagger says and slip the ring on Monica's slender finger.

He hands the other ring to Monica. She has tears in her eyes and a shake in her voice as she repeats after Dagger. "I Monica Gates, take you, Xander Combs, as my husband. To have and to hold, in sickness and in health. With the wellbeing of the Royal Bastards in mind, I will always put you first." She slips the gold band on my finger and adds her own. "Live together, ride together, die together. Forever in my heart, always in my soul."

"With the power vested in me in the state of California and the bylaws of Royal Bastards, I now pronounce you man and wife. You may kiss your bride."

I gather Monica into my arms. "About fucking time." My lips descend upon Monica's hard, kissing her with all the love and passion she pulls out of me. "Welcome to the Royal Bastards, wife."

"Welcome to the Royal Bastards, husband," I growl and kiss her hard again, sealing our lives together forever. No matter what happens, we're in it together.

Capone

6 months later

Nursing a beer in my hand, sitting at the bar in my clubhouse, I watch my sister and her new husband, my VP, Blayze, slow dance to a girly song some club bunny is playing. They're chest to chest. She stares into his eyes, love and adoration shining in her brown depth. A deep pain of longing settles in my chest.

Danyella comes out of the kitchen laughing and joking with Torch, while carrying a tray of food. Her long blonde hair flowing freely down to the center of her back. Anger boils to the surface of my skin and I tamp it down when her blue eyes land on me. She offers me a shy, sweet smile.

A deep ache settles in my chest and the collar of my shirt is choking me. I need air, need to clear my head. Before I can move off the barstool warm, slender nails roughly run through my hair.

My spine stiffens, "I don't know who the fuck is touching me, but if you want to keep your hands, you'll release me now." The anger in my voice is unmistakable.

The nails disappear from my scalp and Rose, a club bunny, presses her fake breasts against my forearm. She bats her fake fucking lashes at me, pursing her red lips into a pout, trying to be seductive. It's pissing me off more than turning me on.

"You look a little tense, Prez. Can I help relieve your stress?"

I think about Rose's offer. It's been months since I've felt the soft curves of a woman. My eyes drift in Danyella's direction on their own accord. Her slender back is facing me and she's watching Dagger and Torch play a game of pool.

God, she's beautiful but stubborn.

My body aches to belong to only her. We've barely talked since we came back from Michigan and that was months ago. The last time I touched those plump lips were after Monica's wedding to Blayze. Things got carried away and before my brain caught up with my aching dick, Danyella and I were in a dark corner, locked in each other's embrace, our lips devouring each other. Her hot breath fanning over my heated skin, moans and whimpers escaping her delicate throat.

Shouts and catcalls pulled me out of my lust induced haze, slamming me back to reality. I stopped Danyella from making a big mistake. My body was screaming at me to continue while my mind was telling me no. I can't defile her beautiful soul with the darkness I carry with me.

After that night, Danyella walked away from me, angry and heartbroken and hasn't looked in my direction since. That is until tonight. Tonight, she's looking at me with lust and longing in her baby blues which are currently staring at me, taking my breath away. She hasn't blessed me with her sweet smile or her light laughter. I don't blame her either. I was a dickhead and deserve it all taken away from me. But damn it, it hurts. I deserve this pain in my chest. All the bad shit I've done. All the blood spilled by my hands. All of it. I don't deserve anything from someone created as an angel.

I shove Rose off me and she falls on her ass with a thud and a cry. I don't even bother to check if she's all right. My boots eat up the distance of the room until I'm in Danyella's space. Her breath catches in her throat but she doesn't break eye contact.

"Belle," I whisper. My breath carrying across her face. "If you're ready for me, be prepared. I won't stop until I have your full submission."

A flush is spreading across her porcelain skin. The music fades away, voices disappear as I stare into her eyes, willing her to give me the green light. Begging her to give in to this attraction we have towards each other.

One word. That's all I need. One word from her plump red lips to put us both out of this misery. Only, that word never comes. Shots ring out through my clubhouse destroying everything in their path.

Want more of Capone? His story will continue in September of 2020.

Thank you

First off, I want to start with my wonderful readers. Thank you for taking the time to read this book. I hope you're enjoying the Royal Bastards MC world.

Crimson and Nikki, thank you for letting me be a part of this world and trusting me to do it right. Without the support behind all the authors in this world, Blayze never would've come to life. So, thank you again for allowing me to be a part of this world.

My Beta Bitches! Joy, Monica, Krista and Sherry. Finding my mistakes and pumping me up for this release. You ladies are my girls and always will be. Thank you for your late-night messages and letting me be a part of your lives. You're forever in mine. Sarah, my Ride or Die. You've been with me since Racing Dirty (even before that with the novels in the vault) Thank you for your editing and feedback on all my work. Without you I would have never pushed that publish button.

Kat, thank you so much for jumping in and proofreading this novel for me. Your feedback was amazing and you did it with a small timeline. Thank you so much for the extra set of eyes! I'm forever indebted to you.

Michelle, oh where to start? We've been together since before Indy publishing (Kind of forced since you're my sister in law) but I wouldn't have it any other way. You're stuck with me for life. Oh! And AARP called, they're still waiting for you to fill out that paperwork.

Rex and my spawns. Each book written is for you. Thank you for putting up with my ass on a daily basis. I love you all from the bottom of my heart.

Lastly, I want to thank my dad. If it wasn't for your love of reading, I never would have pursued doing this. Thank you for your support and undying love of the written word.

Books written by J. Lynn Lombard

Royal Bastards MC

Blayze's Inferno

Amazon: https://amzn.to/2DSLZ1x

Capone's Chaos

Amazon: https://amzn.to/34QUrNS

Capone's Christmas

Amazon: https://amzn.to/34QUrNs

Torch's Torment

Amazon: https://amzn.to/2Vh2Qax

Global Outlaw Syndicate

Deadly Rose:

Amazon: https://amzn.to/3lvyFCt

Savage Saints MC

Kayne's Fury:

Get it here: Amazon: https://amzn.to/2DbXmAl

Blayde's Betrayal

Get it here: Amazon https://amzn.to/2Z0yGoc

Stryker's Salvation

Get it here: Amazon https://amzn.to/2InXZKV

Rooster Redemption and Aces Ascension are coming soon. All are #FreeonKU

Find the stories that started all of this in the completed

Racing Dirty Series

Thrust Amazon: https://amzn.to/2AwrgJ7

Torque (book 2) Amazon: https://amzn.to/2H0JugS

Turbulence (book 3) Amazon: https://amzn.to/2KNuTaj

Made in the USA
Columbia, SC
18 February 2025